BUCK

BUCK

A novel by
BUCK STARR

Made in Charleston, SC
www.PalmettoPublishingGroup.com

Buck

Copyright © 2020 by Buck Starr

All rights reserved

No portion of this book may be reproduced, stored in a retrieval system, or transmitted in any form by any means–electronic, mechanical, photocopy, recording, or other–except for brief quotations in printed reviews, without prior permission of the author.

First Edition

Printed in the United States

ISBN-13: 978-1-64990-112-5
ISBN-10: 1-64990-112-7

CONTENTS

Chapter 1	1
Chapter 2	6
Chapter 3	9
Chapter 4	16
Chapter 5	19
Chapter 6	23
Chapter 7	27
Chapter 8	31
Chapter 9	33
Chapter 10	36
Chapter 11	39
Chapter 12	43
Chapter 13	47
Chapter 14	50
Chapter 15	52
Chapter 16	56
Chapter 17	60
Chapter 18	64
Chapter 19	66
Chapter 20	69
Chapter 21	73
Chapter 22	78
Chapter 23	84
Chapter 24	88
Chapter 25	91
Chapter 26	93
Chapter 27	97
Chapter 28	99
Chapter 29	103
Chapter 30	105

Chapter 31	109
Chapter 32	113
Chapter 33	115
Chapter 34	118
Chapter 35	122
Chapter 36	127
Chapter 37	131
Chapter 38	134
Chapter 39	136
Chapter 40	141
Chapter 41	146
Chapter 42	150
Chapter 43	153
Chapter 44	156
Chapter 45	159
Chapter 46	164
Chapter 47	166
Chapter 48	167
Chapter 49	171
Chapter 50	175
Chapter 51	179
Chapter 52	182
Chapter 53	185
Chapter 54	190
Chapter 55	193
Chapter 56	195
Chapter 57	198
Chapter 58	204
Chapter 59	208
Chapter 60	211
Chapter 61	216
Chapter 62	223
Epilogue	225

CHAPTER 1

No way. That did not just happen.

I'm lined up for the perfect kill shot, and the guy's head explodes in my scope. My target, a middle-Eastern human trafficker who snatched the wrong Sheik's granddaughter, is eliminated. The random thoughts won't stop. Did someone else have a contract on this guy? Did someone steal my contract? Will I get paid anyway? I mean, who's to say that other shot killed him and not mine? My word against the real shooter, and who knows if he'll ever be heard from?

I dismantle and pack up quickly and am in the pickup heading south within 45 seconds. And on the burner immediately.

"Market is down today. Hope your investments are safe".

"Yes. They are right where they should be". Disconnect. Phone goes out the window, never to be traced.

Good. The money will be waiting for me. And I either have a tail or someone else is trying to get out of here using my route. A vehicle is behind me and shouldn't be. So I deviate. A turn on a secondary route

I scouted out last week does the trick. And I get a good look at the other vehicle as it runs past the intersection, still heading south. A grey late-model Jeep Wrangler, nondescript, and the license plate obstructed. The driver is wearing a camo hat and sunglasses, looks to be about mid-thirties, maybe 6', Italian or middle eastern if I had to surmise from the one quick look. I'm guessing that is the shooter. And I'm guessing that I haven't seen or heard the last of him. And how unprofessional? Take the shot when the guy was still in range of collaterals. I mean, I was ready, but two seconds later and the guy would have been clear of his driver and his security as the walkway narrowed. But this guy couldn't wait. Probably hit at least one other person with frags. Where's the pride in that work?

I am not just an assassin. I'm a contract operative. I do more than just kill. But when the job calls for it, I am always crystal clear about who I am engaging and why. No good guys, only bad guys. No children, no women. Call me old fashioned. And no, I do not struggle with guilt over the death of drug lords who poison children, crooked politicians who willingly sacrifice innocent lives for their careers, thugs who make their money selling guns to extremists, and the extremists that use those guns to commit genocide. You get the idea. Vengeance is mine, sayeth the Lord, but perhaps he relies on me, and those like me, to help. I don't pretend to judge them—that is between them and God. To steal an old adage, I just arrange the meeting. I'm okay with that.

And no complaints about living in the shadows either. I like my privacy. I don't like anybody knowing my business. That's why they call it "my" business, right? I like being able to choose where I spend my time and who I spend it with. And I really don't like being told how to live. So this is a good lifestyle for me. I travel when I please. I stay where I want as long as I want. I am unknown, so being in the shadows doesn't mean that I can't go to bars, restaurants, wander the street markets in the Old World. That sort of stuff. Hiding in plain sight, so to speak, because those who see me really see nobody.

Enough about me for now. After going east for about 20 miles, I am able to follow a route south again, and find myself back in the city. This time, it's a European city, one that you would surely recognize if I were to surrender the name. I detour around my hotel for several minutes, checking all the observation points to make sure that it's clear. And it is. I park under a tree in front of a vacant Victorian, three streets away from my hotel, and weave my way to the alley behind the hotel kitchen. With no one close, and nobody watching for me, I slide in the kitchen entrance, slip the manager a bill on the way through, and take the service elevator to the floor above my room. And then I listen for a few minutes. Hearing nothing unusual, I find the west stairway, and walk up two flights, and listen again. Nothing. Go to the east stairwell, down to the floor below mine, and pause to listen one more time. Nothing. Back up the stairs, and a pause at the door to my floor for a minute. Then the short walk to my room, and a stop at my door to check for tampering. Into the room. Everything in place, no sounds that worry me. Good. Time for a drink.

I pour a bourbon into a tumbler (it's a nice hotel) and take a swallow. Very nice stuff. I'm not one of those who commiserate over a drink. When I want one, I get one. It's neither bad nor good; it's just a drink. Between me and the bottle, as it were. And if I choose to have a lot of them, no biggie. I'm a spiritual person, but I think God has bigger things to worry about than whether or not I have a drink once in a while.

I remove my nano laptop from its hiding place. I made it look like the floor vent. Even if someone removed the vent to see if anything was hidden in the duct, they'd be holding the computer while they were looking, and then would put it right back into the hiding place. Good recon makes for good hiding places. I checked this hotel out a few days before the job and had a geek in a neighboring Country build the components into a model of the floor vent.

I set the vent/computer onto the charging pad, and pull out my phone. The phone allows me to access to the nano, and the data appears on my screen. All wireless. Most of what I need can be done on my phone anyway, but there are times that I need the additional features the nano gives me. Today is one such time. My phone doesn't have the capacity to navigate all the cyber challenges necessary to access the bank account, which is fine. It stays safer from stray eyes that way. The deposit is made and pending validation. When you are as reliable as me, the client doesn't have to wait for a second confirmation of your work. When you tell them it's done, it's done. And I get the money without delay. It pays, literally, to have a solid reputation. I suppose it doesn't hurt that everyone I deal with knows that I could kill them if they fucked me. Not that I would ever do that.

This payment is tentative. Not sure yet if I'll keep it. I need to know the deal with the other shooter.

I check my super-secret website. Two jobs await my decision. An assassination in Iraq and a sting in the Greek Isles. I like the one in the Greek Isles, mostly because it is one of my favorite places on earth. And it involves an interesting woman. It doesn't appear that anyone is going to get killed, an upside when you can get it. Usually there are no G-men looking to get you when no one actually dies. I mean, criminals don't report lost guns or lost drugs or the theft of dirty money. And they don't like admitting that they got swindled or out-foxed. But bodies lying around tend to draw attention. So I indicate my acceptance through a complicated series of clicks and dropdown menus, close down the computer, and return it to vent status for now. When I leave for Greece, the nano will be destroyed. A bit of a waste, but an expense that I figure into every job.

I settle in to relax and ponder. The drink is good, and my enjoyment of it only mildly reduced because of the thoughts of the other shooter. I may encounter them again, and I want no more surprises. My serenity depends on knowing what's going to happen. And I am very selfish about my serenity. I have no room for the unknown. I have to find out more. So I slam back the last of the drink and set out.

CHAPTER 2

I find a little cafe about a two mile walk from the hotel. I haven't eaten here. I try not to go the same place twice when on a job. The longer jobs sometimes dictate that I hit a place more than once, but I'll do so at different times and keep the visits as far apart as possible. After a fresh whitefish on a bed of seasoned rice and two martinis—like tits, one's not enough, three's too many—I grab a cab and have him take me to the hotel district. I almost never stay in a hotel district, because, well, people from all over tend to be around there, and people from all over could be people that I have run into before. I don't need that. I like to stay in isolated hotels, or rent-by-month apartments. Or even hostels now and then, when I need to get some local information.

It's late enough now and the crowds on the street have thinned, so I cruise the parking lots and parking garages for 25 minutes, and sure enough, there is the Jeep. The sticker on the front windshield reveals that it is a rental from the airport. And it's parked in the valet section of the Hilton. Absolutely no imagination.

Could anybody be dumb enough to shoot someone and then drop their car off with a valet? Where's the weapon? In a hidden compartment in the Jeep? Or did he carry a disassembled sniper rifle up to the room with him in a violin case or something? And is he really that stupid to not only telegraph that he is in the area, but actually give away which hotel he is in? I can't believe that anybody in this line of work is that clueless. So I keep investigating.

The Marriott across the street has a business center, and I hop on one of the computers. I send a message to another geek I know, and she sends me back a list of the room occupants of the Hilton in about 30 minutes. My geeks are really good. And this particular one happens to also be a knockout. That's what us old guys used to call a hot woman back in the day. She hasn't wasted her advanced degree from Ohio State either. She is a full professor of IT or cyber security or some such discipline there. What a great cover. Hopefully driving that Ferrari won't draw too much suspicion to her side pursuits.

She has gone to the trouble of annotating by every name whether they are obviously legitimate or not. No wonder it took her 30 minutes. She has a sixth sense about requests like this and in this case, as usual, it takes a lot of the guess work out of my next step. There are only three unknowns in the entire hotel, so I start with them. With some googling and historical searches, I find out that one of the names is likely a lady who is having a little tryst. She is from here, and rents hotel rooms out locally every couple of weeks. One name is mysterious in that there is no history whatsoever. But the third, well, that is probably my guy. Even though I suspect the name is a fraud, he seems to have used it before. That means he has a fake passport or some other fake ID that carries this fake name. He has travelled from Kuwait under the name at least twice in the past four months, and stayed in hotels in the same cities as my target here did, in the same general time frames as the target. A little more surfing and Viola!, the fake passport. The picture could very easily be the guy that I saw in the Jeep. The hat and glasses don't help, but there is something about seeing a guy and then seeing him again. And this seemed like him. I shop the picture around a number of sites and come up with a match. While the name is fairly common in Kuwait, the address tells it all. Remember the Sheik? This guy is one of the granddaughter's uncles, which I know from my preparatory research. He spent time in the Kuwaiti Military. Likely had the skills to pull off that shot, but not a pro. Shit. I can't keep the entire fee. So out of what little honor remains of my character, I will return half of the fee. Keep enough to cover my expenses and a little pocket change. But I cannot begrudge a family member the taste of revenge. They deserve it. The Sheik, while richer than God, shouldn't be paying in full for a service that his son gave for free. Mystery solved and overall I feel rather good about it. Scumbag gets to go to the devil and be told "Oh, BTW, the uncle did you in and laughed about it all the way home. Now strip down and jump in that fire over there". And I get $1.5 mil. Just another day at the office.

CHAPTER 3

I decide to take the long way to Greece, since I have plenty of time. Flying gets me on cameras and burns passports. Driving and busses and trains and hopping boats can be almost anonymous when used correctly. So I drive the pickup to the eastern European border, ditch it, and get a train ticket to Plovdiv, Bulgaria. The truck won't cause any problems. If anyone checked it out when it was found, the farthest they would get would be a birth certificate and headstone of a dude that lived and died in Montreal. I score a private cabin on the train and catch up on my sleep. You never know when you'll have to stay awake for 48 hours, so catching 8 straight hours of sleep is always welcome. From Plovdiv I take a bus down to Petrich—that was the easy part. I had decided it best to forge a walking path across the border into Greece. Petrich is on the eastern edge of the Belasica Mountains, and the terrain is no picnic. So even though Fort Roupel, Greece was close—only about 25 klicks—the walk would be difficult since I would need to divert off the roads the last two or three miles in Bulgaria and the first couple in

Greece. Fort Roupel would have a bus to the coast of the Aegean Sea—more specifically, Thessaloniki. So I get off the bus in Petrich, and stop at a local mehane—fancy Bulgarian word for a bar—to have a meal and a Carlsberg. I have the meshana skara, which is basically just a lot of Bulgarian meat. Refueled, I start the walk. No reason I shouldn't make it in under four hours, even with the rough terrain.

The weather sucks—damp and cold—but my estimate holds, and I get to Fort Roupel at about dark. A bus runs the late route down to Thessaloniki, so I buy a fare and get on my way. Less than two hours direct, it takes nearly five hours because of the many stops along the way. I catch some good sleep. In Thessaloniki, I rent out a fishing boat to take me to the waters south of Greece and let me off on the mainland. Then, I hoof it again, putting distance between the port and my next human contact. I catch a ride with a commercial trucker at a Greek taverna after having local falafel, and he takes me to the shore closest to my destination island—an Isle that you would certainly recognize were I to provide the name. I catch a ferry to the island, and the pleasurable part of this trip begins. I take in the beauty of the waters around the Greek Isles. Incomparable.

Now that I have reached paradise, I find the apartment I pre-booked after a considerable internet search. It fits my needs and provides some extra benefits as well. Rather isolated, grand view, and comfortable. Rents by the month, and the transaction was blind. They asked for pre-payment with a credit card and I asked for the keys to be left where I could find them without having to meet with anyone. After offering them 20% more rent, they agreed to leave the keys in a planter on the balcony by the front door. As I planned, the taxi dropped me off two days after my rental contract began. I had him take me to a taverna that I had checked out on the web. It was about four blocks from the apartment. I did my recon, walking around the neighborhood, going past the apartment and checking out the areas around it until I was sure that no one was staking the place out. I stop in a convenient store and buy some necessities—wine, bourbon, cigars, pastries—and head to the apartment.

Finally, I enter. It is furnished as expected, vacation-rental common. Chairs with wooden arms, fake Persian rugs covering the floors, but comfortable—and a great view of the water from the balcony. Time to relax. Tomorrow the recon would begin.

I find a glass and pour myself a bourbon from the bottle I just purchased. I measure the kitchen cabinets, and email a friend the specs. My new nano component will pose as a shelf in a kitchen cabinet. I make arrangements to pick it up under the fourth pew from the front, on the right side of the sanctuary, of the biggest cathedral in Athens. Four days later, I make the day-long trip there and back, and now I have the access I need to track the information I will need. Whatever that may turn out to be.

Recon is best completed at a slow pace. The natural events don't always occur within a day or two. Weekly festivals, the regulars that come in from out-of-town, the weather patterns of the period; none of this can be accurately gauged in a few days. So for the next several weeks, I roam the island, and those nearby, eating and drinking and enjoying the sights as a common, nondistinct tourist. And although Greek food is not my favorite, the local fish is always a hit with me. So I enjoy fresh fish, even though the names of them are literally Greek to me. I mean, even the lobster in Greece isn't called lobster. They call it astakos or something like that. But I was eating very well. Although immensely popular in Greece, I don't drink ouzo, because I don't care for black licorice. But the wine industry in Greece has developed well, and that did quite nicely for me.

I spent some evenings on my western-shore apartment looking out over the water, the experience often enhanced by a fine Corona cigar in one hand and a bourbon or red in the other. The view there is indescribable. I was fortunate enough to land an apartment on one of the stair-step plateaus rising up a couple of hundred feet from the beach. Sitting there in the light breeze, watching what may be the most beautiful sunset anywhere, I would take account of my situation in as realistic terms as possible for a person of my profession. Thankfully I don't battle with wretched feelings about what I do or how I live. I was a good son. I took care of my parents when they were alive, and saw them often. In fact, I don't remember a time when they were alive that I didn't go stay with them in between jobs. Of course, I was much more protected then because I was an employee of a government agency, so they were never in danger because of me or what I did. It was only after they passed—one within a year of the other just like they always predicted—that I strapped on the more anonymous, and I suppose more dangerous, way of doing business. I was an only child, and never married, and never sired an offspring, so I am autonomous in the familial regard. Perfect for what I do. I don't even have girlfriends for much longer than a job takes, and I can't remember the last woman that knew my real name.

My prep time was uneventful, except for one evening when I ventured to the mainland and went several miles inland to check out a taverna I had heard was worth the trip. And it was. The fish was awesome, prepared with some type of marinade that brought all the fresh sweetness out of the meat. And the scenery was made for a single guy in every respect. The setting was almost tropical, and the ladies were encouraging and chatty. I was having a cabernet at the fancy wine bar after dinner, and enjoying conversation with a local maiden, when it became clear that another patron had eyes for her. In fact, it seemed he envisioned himself as the only guy for her. Judging by the reactions around the bar, he asserted himself as such regularly. When he approached me, and it was clear that his intent was not necessarily to make a new friend, people began moving away. It was obvious that none of them wanted anything to do with his ire. Innocent bystanders: none willing to stop him but none willing to join him. As usual, I was on my own. Just as I preferred it.

I saw him peripherally as he strode across the bar. I think the fact that he made no attempt to hide his angst, and the crowd literally parted as he walked through them, gave away his intentions. His first sound was, predictably, "Hey!". A Mensa candidate. I turned just slightly enough to allow that I heard him and was just glancing to see who he may be talking to. He cleared that up immediately, albeit predictably once again, with his "I'm talking to you Kamaki" declaration. Now I don't speak Greek, but I know that "Kamaki" means this guy thought I was flirting with his alleged girlfriend.

"Thanks for the invite, but I am already engaged in conversation with this nice lady. Can I get back to you in a while?"

He stopped, and you could almost see the wheels turning in his head, thinking what was the matter with this foreigner talking to my woman and brushing me aside like this?

"Well, your conversation is over".

"Artemus don't start. You must stop doing this."

Aha. One person wasn't scared of old Artie. The woman he worshipped.

"No Kamaki wanted here." He was less enraged, softened by her reprimand, but the zone was not yet clear. "You leave now, or I will help you leave".

Not bad English, but English is commonly spoken here. "Sure thing. In fact, the lady and I were just leaving." I turned to her. "Shall we?"

I think that was just too much for Artie. He was big, about 6'3', broad, and in good shape. Likely worked labor on a boat or in a mine. Younger than me, but gave the impression that he isn't very smart. And hearing me say that I was going to waltz out of there with his "lady" put him over the edge. His ego wasn't having that. So he made his move. Unfortunately for him, as established prior, he was predictable. When he began moving his arm to formulate some type of offensive attack, I jabbed his throat with my knuckles and broke his nose with the heel of my hand. Just a flash of compact movement, probably not even seen by many of the folks in the bar. Left, right. Just like marching in the Army. And he was on his knees, coughing and gagging, trying to catch his breath without breathing through his ruined nose. Tough times. I leaned over and whispered, so as to not embarrass him, "I think we'll be going now, just as you suggested. Have a pleasant evening". And thankfully, I saved some face, because she actually went with me. The evening got much better after that.

When I left that neighborhood early the next morning, I had to put it on my list of places to stay away from henceforth. I had made too much of an impression and couldn't risk being remembered.

CHAPTER 4

The time was drawing near. I was commissioned to meet and become friendly with what was, but a short time ago, a distant heir to the throne of Musjistan, a small kingdom bordered on the west by Russia and south by the Caspian Sea. They controlled nothing but their little Country, but there was enough oil to keep them viable as a civilization. In short, their citizens worked and lived and were, for the most part, living their lives without starvation or tyranny. And there is something to be said for that in certain regions of the world. This heir was a single woman, young but mature, and recent events had turned her status from "distant" heir to "imminent" heir. The King had died suddenly, and his son, the heir-apparent, had abdicated his entitlement in favor of marrying a woman from the UAE. They met as many Royals do, through mutual Royal acquaintances, and he fell deeply in love with her riches. For while she was not close to being a ruling deity in Abu Dhabi, she was wealthier than the fortunes of the throne in Musjistan, by a hundred times. So his attraction was immediate, and she was blinded by love, as it were. As if these circumstances were not odd enough, the next person in line to the throne, the King's daughter, made the mistake of traveling to the UK to check on her investments, and was promptly arrested for drug smuggling by Scotland Yard. Apparently, the prospect of being number three to the throne did not interest her as much as investing in a prosperous cocaine venture with her younger brother, who was the fourth in line for the throne. After she was arrested, the whole story came out, and while she only suffered life imprisonment in London, her brother suffered banishment from the Country for embarrassing the Crown; effectively disqualifying his claim to the throne in the process. Per the Musjistan Charter of Royalty, which laid out the rather convoluted and confusing lineage of the throne, the current ruler was now the last remaining sibling of the departed King: the aging Grandfather of the young Heiress. With the parents having died from the Musjistanian plague of 1999, there remained no relatives between the Grandfather and the subject Heiress. She was now directly in line: no siblings to muddy the ascendancy. But there was a cousin, Ta, a son of the second oldest female sibling of the King, who, had she lived long enough, would have then succeeded the King; but the cousin's path deviated by the fact that his mother was deceased. So the Crown was bestowed upon the remaining sibling due to the path of ascendancy provided by the Charter of Royalty, thus putting the young Heiress as the direct descendent, and not her now-distressed cousin. Complete bummer for the aspiring cousin. Older than her, he was unhappy with the prospect of never becoming King, and equally unhappy with idea that she would squander away the fortunes of the Crown with benevolent acts of charity towards the citizens. For that is exactly what she said she would do if ever she became Queen. And cousin Ta was having none of that, which is where I come in.

My role was to befriend the Heiress, christened "Jules" by her late parents, and prevent her assassination. While doing so, I was also to discredit the cousin to the extent that he would be banished from the Kingdom, thereby removing the threat of his insurgency not just for now, but forever. Befriending Jules should not be hard since she was not well known at all, and not even considered a celebrity by the rest of the world. She could travel in relative anonymity, and was doing just that on a month-long vacation to the Greek Isles. Unbeknownst to her, the jealous cousin Ta was plotting her untimely death during her vacation. Killing her outside of Musjistan had benefits for him. If he could do so without the normally ineffective Greek Hellenic Police quickly solving the crime, he would become the Crown Prince, after which he could squelch any suspicions in his own Country. After all, who would dare mess with the direct heir to the throne of an aging King? Stopping him and discrediting him were seemingly the more difficult parts of the mission.

CHAPTER 5

The now-Princess Jules arrived on schedule, departing from her first class cabin without fanfare. Apparently the Royal jet was not available. I first saw her as she moved gracefully down the stairs to the tarmac, the airport not having the gate to accommodate any commercial jets. She was better than her pictures in every aspect. But both belied her ancestry. The people of Musjistan and the surrounding region possessed mostly eastern European features. Jules was a dark beauty. She looked more like a Latina: long dark hair, tan skin, dark eyes. I wasn't close enough yet to tell, but those eyes looked raven from my vantage point in the terminal. I had purchased a cheap fare under one of my identities so I could get through security and watch the party as they deplaned. I didn't expect anything to go down there, but I wanted to be as close as possible, as much as possible, until such time as I knew more about Ta's scheme. I could also maybe catch any nuances emitted from the group as they first arrived. Which I did. I don't know how everyone acts or thinks in Muji—the accepted short form of the Country name—but for sure, the entourage with Jules worshipped her. And her security team were no slouches. They were alert and looked like pros. I counted three of them. This supported my intel: The Crown was not aware of Ta's plans. Since Muji had no permanent military, the security escorts trained in Russia and Turkey, their closest allies. They should be good. The rest of the travel party were attentive to her and her needs, anticipating her every move, and acting as if they were damn lucky just to be near her. I got that. With just a glance, anyone could see that she was something special.

The Crown was not aware of the threat to the Princess because the source of the intel was the Turkish Secret Intelligence Corps (SIC). Being the most unstable country in the region, Turkey felt the need to create the best intelligence network possible. And they did. They may not win any wars, but they were sure that they would know if one was coming. Through their constant efforts to protect Turkey from the threat of aggression from middle eastern states, one day they uncovered communications that indicated a need for certain types of weaponry for an attack in the Greek Isles. They worked the lead hard, and found out that this attack was possibly being planned to appear to be a preemptory strike by Iran, to avert some sort of planned Greek offensive: A prima-facie false premise to those on the inside of the intelligence circle, because Iran would have nothing to do with anything like that. Even Iranian leaders, as ignorant as they are, know that Greece would not actually attack. Greece would get annihilated by just about anyone. Except maybe Muji.

Another possibility was for the strike to look like a terrorist act.

It was all coming from inside Musjistan. The cousin had been shopping for weaponry big enough to leave the impression that another small country attacked Greece. But while Royalty has it's perks, it does not guarantee brains. So Ta got a little careless and one of his communiques were intercepted by Turkey and, since it referenced Iran and weapons, the Turkish latched onto it like a tick onto a logger's head. They watched and followed the communications until they verified the source as Muji. They used some of their diplomatic force to sniff around inside of Musjistan, and got a break when one of Ta's confidants slipped up. Just slightly. What he thought was a well-masked inference about "Island delights" and "fireworks" in a private email to Ta, instead became the confirmation of the source. Muji possessed no island. And in the history of the Country, there had never been a fireworks display. Some innocent questions to those closest to the Crown drew puzzled denials about islands and fireworks. That closed the deal. And Ta was none the wiser. SIC stayed on the trail until they pieced together Ta's grand plan: To obtain weapons of war, deploy them against Greece, and ensure that the Princess was killed during the attacks. They elected not to inform the King for worry of discourse in Muji and a slight fear that he could possibly have some involvement. Ta was close to the King, and His Majesty may not believe such a fantastic story. It was rumored that the King was concerned about the Princess' plans for the fortunes of the Crown, and was using back-door channels to try to rally public support for her to change her thinking. The SIC feared that maybe the dislike of his heiress, combined with his favoritism towards Ta, might tempt the King to react in a not-so-royal fashion; or worse yet, may have prompted him to be a part of the plot. So they elected to try to stop the madness themselves. The international intelligence community has network after network of clandestine communication channels. My website was as dark as they came. But if a person has access to any of the major intelligence websites, they can find operatives to do their dirty work for them. And that's where the Turks went.

Enter me. Yep, they called Buck.

CHAPTER 6

I learned that Ta was not on the island yet. He was being tracked by my client, and they still had him in Muji. But he was coming. He wanted to be on the island with Jules when the attack occurred, to somehow divert accusations that maybe he had something to do with her demise. He would then escort her remains back to the Motherland, posing as the grieving cousin who just wished it had been him instead of her; and wished that he could have done something to save her; blah blah blah. What a dick. I was kind of wishing that this was just an assassination after all. He would be an incredibly satisfying kill.

Meanwhile, the Princess had started her vacation. My movement was free here, so I could watch her with relative ease. My craft was not needed so much because I was both unknown and unremarkable, and at this point I was without resistance or conflict. I took precautions, and would always be able to tell if someone had been in the apartment. But otherwise, I roamed the island like a buffalo on the open range—something I wasn't able to do on many jobs. It felt good.

The Princess liked the beach, and I liked it when she went there—impeccable taste in bikinis. She favored simple food. She preferred food carts on the streets and out-of-the-way tavernas. A woman after my own heart, as they say. I had a number of different strategies to meet her in a non-threatening way, but wanted to be sure that she felt like she was initiating the meeting; not me. That took a little more planning. But as sometimes happens, I got lucky.

It happened the first full weekend of her stay. Hard to distinguish it was a weekend, because every day feels like a weekend on the Greek isles. As usual, I was in her outer atmosphere as she made her way around the island. Just keeping tabs, learning her habits, likes, dislikes, whatever I could learn. On this particular day, she was working the outdoor markets pretty hard, and because this limited my orbit to a smaller areas, I had to be careful not to be seen too often. I took up residency at a cabana-type café next to the market she was in. It allowed me to see three of the four perimeters of the market. I treated myself to a local beer; a name I will never attempt to pronounce, but not a bad beer. I wasn't too concerned that she would leave the market without me seeing her, because it would be simple enough finding her at the next one if in fact she did. I was wearing a Reds baseball hat and Revos, black trunks and a white Columbia fishing shirt; and not looking too much out of place—only mildly so. In a place as wonderful as this, all sorts of people come from all sorts of places, and most of us look at least a little out of place. So no one really pays attention.

I watched the market. The boundary of shop closest to me was defined by dress after dress hanging all across the back of it. Suddenly the most beautiful Princess ever to wear a crown emerged from this wall of dresses. Jules had parted the hanging textiles and walked out of the shop directly towards me. She was just a yard or so away, and I had no way of moving without it looking like I was trying to get away from her. She sat right beside me and looked at my glass.

"That beer looks so refreshing. What kind is it?"

"You'll really have to ask the bartender—I couldn't pronounce it on a bet." Her smile said that she might have thought that my ignorance was a little amusing.

"Fine. Bartender Sir, I shall have the same as Mr. umm…."

"Buck". I said. "No Mr. Just Buck". I told myself that it was fine to use my real name. I mean, she's a Princess, right?

"Jules. So nice to make your acquaintance" she said while offering her delicate hand. She was nothing if not eloquent. I returned the gesture and thought I felt a little electric pulse go through me when she clasped my hand. "I'll have the same as Mr. Buck here, please."

Her beer came and I offered a toast to her and the weather. Both were beautiful. And we were off.

"So are you on Holiday?" She politely queried.

"Yes I am. You?"

"Yes. I am from Musjistan. You probably know it as Muji. That's what they call it around here. And you, where are you from?"

"United States. You probably know it as America. That's what they call it around here". She actually laughed. My, am I witty today.

The conversation went on from there. She never mentioned that she was Royalty. She introduced her two shopping escorts as "friends"; said nothing about the two security guys keeping watch. She probably figured I didn't notice them.

Conversation with her was easy. She talked as if she had nothing on her mind but today, and like there were no worries that could ruin life. She was optimistic, intelligent, and a generous conversationalist. I liked her immediately. We sat there for two beers and I still felt like there was a lot left in the conversation if we had taken the time.

I am not nearly as handsome as I think I am, but she agreed to meet me for dinner anyway. And that is how I met the Princess.

CHAPTER 7

I inventoried my kit and weapons that afternoon. It had been a couple of days, and I never like to go too long without checking. Everything was there, exactly as I left it. Always good to know that I can protect myself or bug out at any time without delay. I like to think that's how I have stayed alive this long. But it's probably just luck. Like meeting the Princess out of the blue.

I was feeling a little anxious. Or maybe nervous, I don't know. Was this a date to her? Or just a bored woman on the island looking for a little different company than her entourage? Not really important because it was all part of the plan for me. The important thing was that I could now work on getting her a little closer and building some trust so she won't freak out because I'm around. I debated taking the Glock with me to supper. The flight from Muji to Greece was pretty short, and feasibly, Ta could get here before I really knew he had left. So the Glock won the debate and went along for the ride. The truth is, I often pretend to debate myself on whether or not to take the gun with me—but it always goes. It's just a thing I go through to make myself feel a little more normal than I am. Like it's a choice that people make every day. The fact is, there is no choice. The Glock is always with me.

The Princess selected an attractive scarlet summer dress for the evening, accented with a grey clutch and matching heels. A modest gold necklace topped off the combo. She was stunning in every way. I needed to act cool, so my acting skills were going to be tested; inside, I was far from cool.

I picked a small taverna on the mainland for drinks and a meal. It was well off the beaten path and far away from the place I met Artie. It was really a local place, but no town is big enough to keep all the tourists away. Some of them search for the local places to enhance their vacation experience. I had been there a couple of times since I had been in Greece, and it was my favorite. The inside was old-style Greek décor, and comfortable. I made a point not to go to any one place often enough to become known. I was appreciating that craft tonight because this was just the kind of place the Princess liked. So the evening was great, all of it: Food, company, drinks, and the entertainment was a guy with a guitar with a real talent for classical music. Her security guys sat conspicuously inconspicuous at a corner table that gave them views of the front door, the hallway to the back, and us. They were dressed casual enough to blend as much as most vacationers do, and they even put off a little nuance that they might be a couple. Nice touch, I thought. So far I was impressed with their work.

The Princess appreciated chivalry—she asked me to order for her. We both had the spetsiota, a baked fish repast. I could tell it had tomatoes, garlic, and wine, and I'm sure there were some secret spices or something in it. But it was delightful. We enjoyed it with a bottle of a crisp chardonnay.

Just when I thought things couldn't go better, the ferry ride back to the island proved me wrong. The breeze was refreshing, not too cool, but she shivered a bit and I gave her my sport coat. We stood at the rail, watching the lights from the island as they came to us. As we stood there holding the rail, she laid her hand on mine and gave it a soft squeeze. "Tonight has been so nice. And you are quite the gentleman".

"You must be running with a bad crowd. Where I'm from, we hold women in high regard".

"Where I'm from, people hold me in high regard because they think they have to. Kind of takes the luster off of it."

"What do you mean?" I think I she is about to confess to her greatness.

"Now don't laugh, but I am a Princess in Muji." I couldn't help but smile, but I still gave her a disbelieving look, for effect. "No really, I am. It's not that big of a deal. I mean, we are a small country."

"A Princess, huh? No bull, really?"

"Really."

"So should I be bowing or kissing your ring or something?"

She smiled again, but an edge creeped into her voice. "Please, no. Don't do anything like that. I hated to even tell you because I don't want things to change between us. But I would hate even more to keep something like this from you. You would find out soon enough, and when you do, I don't want you to resent that I wasn't completely forthcoming."

"You worry too much. I can't see myself ever being upset with you. But I do appreciate the consideration, Your Highness" I smirked.

That got me a playful punch to the shoulder. "C'mon Buck. Don't ruin a good thing".

"It is a pretty good thing, isn't it?"

She moved in a little closer and I sure enjoyed the rest of the boat ride.

CHAPTER 8

The next day saw the beginning of a pattern that put me right where I needed to be. Every day for the next week, she would call, we would meet somewhere for breakfast or tea, or maybe take a mid-morning walk, and then hit the markets or beaches or even take a boat around the islands. We'd break for a few hours to get ready for the evening and then meet up for dinner. Some days her "friends" would roll with us; some days they would not. On the days they did not, she was becoming more and more affectionate, and I wasn't having any issue with that. The last night together of that week, she decided to end the evening with a rather passionate kiss. Being the expert operative I am, I made her believe that I liked it as much as she did. Took almost no effort.

Jules vacation was nearing the expiration date. She was starting the third week and Ta hadn't made his move. Intelligence said that he was still in Muji. Jules was making my life enjoyable in just about every respect, and her aides were becoming more and more scarce as the days passed. But her security guys, although now working one per shift since they had evaluated every local threat to the fullest, were always close by. The check they ran on me was detailed, to include background, work history, financial, relatives, acquaintances; like applying for the Secret Service. It had all been fabricated and backed up with sources and documents, clear back to my alleged birth date. So there were no cracks. Had to be that way with an alias, or people get dead. People like me.

My cover work was as an independent real estate broker. I charmed Jules with a little knowledge about some of the local properties, just to make it authentic. The homework on that was easy, but you would have thought I invented real estate the way she hung on every lying word. In real life, I don't lie unless someone gets too inquisitive about my work. But lying to a gorgeous princess in order to save her life left me with no guilt whatsoever. In the end, I hope she lives to be mad at me for a long, long time. She's definitely a life worth saving.

I got word on the Thursday of her third week that Ta was on the way. He called Jules and told her that he needed some relaxation and thought he would come down and hang out. She seemed fine with it, but you could tell that he was not her favorite person. She confided in me that he was okay, he was a relative, and that he was not excited about her plans when she took over the throne. In fact, she said, they had heated conversations over it, and she had stuck to her guns. It was this same conversation wherein she shared that she was next in line for the throne and he one below her. I acted surprised again.

CHAPTER 9
Damascus, two months prior

Ta was making his move to buy munitions for his fake attack. Finally, he had got a contact that he was told had the goods. And the call was made. The Lebanese arms merchant had little interest in this deal, but he had a reputation to protect, so he took the meeting. Ta had nearly $500,000 Euros to make a deal. In his small mind, that was enough to arm an entire brigade. He was in for a shocker.

"So you want a light recon plane, with the missiles intact. And four extra missiles and mounts for the plane. And as many bombs as you can get that could be dropped from that plane?"

"Yes, that is correct.". Ta could feel the excitement building. At last he was getting somewhere.

"Here's the deal. We have one decommissioned light recon plane with the missiles intact, but only two extra missiles and mounts. The only bombs I can come up with that could be dropped from a plane are some old WWII bombs that France made. Not very powerful; nothing like the Germans or the Yanks were making. But they are bombs."

"That will do. How much?"

"Let's see. Seven million Euros for the plane, and everything else for another two million. That's going to give you four missiles and two bombs and a delivery system for them. Pretty good deal".

Nine million Euros? Was this guy nuts? "Not nine million. Too much for this old merchandise. I'll give you a half million for everything".

"When is the last time you bought a bomb? 1945? Half a million maybe buys you one bomb and one missile, and I could only give you that price if you're buying the plane too."

"It's too much. What else do you have?"

"Tell me what you're trying to do, and what your budget is, and maybe I can tell you what I have that will help".

"I want the appearance of an outside invasion—one country to another. I want it targeted to a specific area, with the assurance that everyone in the target area will die. I need to do this for $500,000 Euro."

The merchant was a little surprised by the candor, but he had dealt with the ruthless elements of society many times before. So he took it in stride.

"What is the target radius?"

"A building, maybe 2000 square feet."

"I can get you RPGs and mortars with launchers. $50 thousand Euros each. They will destroy a designated target of that size from 500 yards to a mile away with little to no collateral damage outside of the target area." He was being very generous about the 500 yards—that was an absolute maximum range for an RPG, and that would be only with a very experienced shooter.

"They will have to do. I'll take two of each."

The lack of questions about the which of the weapons were stronger, which had the better range, and which had the more exact targeting further confirmed to the merchant that he was dealing with a rank amateur. "Yes Sir. When do you want to take delivery?"

"In six weeks. And I want them delivered offshore, close to Greece."

"We can make that happen. We have shipping vessels that work with us. Half the money up front, the remainder upon delivery. Everything sent to the account numbers I give you."

"Don't I need the names of the banks?"

"No. I will give you a web address and an account number. That is all you will need to transfer the money. When can I expect the first installment?"

"Tomorrow. I want this done." Ta stood, nodded to the merchant, and left Lebanon, hoping he would never have to go back there.

CHAPTER 10
Musjistan, two weeks later

"The missiles will be delivered the third week of Jules' vacation. No reason for us to go there earlier. Mistaf, how close are you?"

His beleaguered assistant was worn to the bone with Ta's obsession. But he knew that this plan would put him in the Palace if it worked. And everyone wanted to be in the Palace. "I have continued to read all the literature and have watched every video available on the RPGs and mortar launchers. We should have no problems destroying our target."

"Should?" Ta's anger was at the surface. "Should, you say? We must know for sure that the missiles will hit the target. There can be no mistakes."

"Yes, my Prince. I will keep learning. I will be the preeminent expert by the time we fire the missiles."

"Good. Now go. I have some calls to make."

Mistaf shuffled out of the room. He was loyal, but Ta did not think he had the brains to ever be anything but his gopher. He did have an innate sense of weaponry, though. Kind of a savant thing. And Ta was counting on that to get the job done.

Ta called the Palace and asked for a meeting with the King. It was granted, and he was there in minutes.

An aide met Ta at the front entrance of the Palace and walked him through the massive structure. The King seldom let visitors roam the Palace unless they were very close family. Ta was family, but known to be a bit spurious. So Ta was escorted to a parlor. The King was taking his meetings there today, surrounded by advisors, as was the norm. "Ta, my son, how are you?"

"I am well, my King. And how is His Majesty?"

"As well as can be expected for an old man. And what brings you to see me today?"

"I would have a suggestion that may help protect the Crown." Ta had to be careful here; he didn't want the King to see through this charade.

"By all means, let's have it."

Ta choose his words carefully. "I am worried about Jules. She has planned a long vacation despite her increased duties in the Kingdom. She is the direct heir to the throne. She needs to learn the part. God forbid, if anything happens to you, she will be sorely unprepared to manage the Kingdom." Ta cringed as he waited for the King's reply.

"I understand. I have the same worries. She is bright and willing, but she believes that she can run the Kingdom her way, without respecting the old ways. She sees the wealth of the Crown as something that belongs to every citizen. Her heart is firmly in the right place; but her head refuses to see the bigger picture. She needs to learn and understand what it takes to run the Kingdom. Experience will teach her. What would you have me do?"

"If I may be so presumptuous, I think she needs to be assigned tasks that will expose her to the world views that are so important to know when running an entire Kingdom." He was almost there.

"What do you have in mind?"

"Jules is going to be on her Greek holiday when the Coronation of the new Greek Cardinal will occur. Several Greek dignitaries and Cardinals from the Vatican will be at the coronation. Since she will already be in Greece, maybe she should attend the ceremony as your emissary? After all, we have petitioned the Church to appoint a Cardinal for Musjistan. It couldn't hurt for the Pope to know that you sent an emissary all the way to the Greek Isles to celebrate the appointment there."

"You may be on to something there Ta. Let me consider this. Anything else?"

"No Your Majesty. Just thinking how monumental it would be for you to be the King that finally got Musjistan recognized by the Pope. Every King before you has tried and failed."

"Monumental. Yes." The hook was set.

The King sent Ta on his way and turned to his advisors. They gave astute audience, as always. "Find out exactly when Jules will be in Greece and put together a list of some possible duties for her there. The Greeks are friends—let's take advantage of her trip."

And the minions scattered to do his bidding.

CHAPTER 11
Today, back in the isles

The water in the Greek Isles is a deep blue/green, yet so clear. The flora is unmatched, even by that in Japan and Costa Rica, in my opinion. Not as plentiful, but what there is stands above the rest of the world. Depending on the island, you can find white beaches, shell beaches, red beaches, black beaches, or tan beaches. Breathtaking scenery abounds in every direction: the hills and mountains, the beaches and ocean, the architecture and flowers. So it came as no surprise that, in the evenings, the Princess and I would sometimes walk up the winding roads above the ocean, just to catch the breeze and the views. And talk, or not talk. Whatever mood struck us. The relationship was solidifying, and my cover was holding up well; turns out I am a convincing as a charming real estate agent. The mission was moving forward just as planned.

I should have known things were going too well.

On our stroll last evening, we came upon a man and woman in a heated exchange. Him in a dark suit with his tie loosened, her in a white summer dress. He was being physical, wrenching her wrists and jerking her violently, both of them screaming: him in anger, her in pain. Right there on the stone sidewalk in front of a little bar.

"Hey pal". I couldn't help myself. "Ease up there, okay?"

"Fuck off." An American. Great for our image.

"I'd rather see you just let her go."

"I said fuck off." I don't think he liked me.

"Look, you need to let her go, and you need to do that now." I couldn't fool around with this drunk too long. She was in pain.

"Are you deaf or stupid? For the last time, fuck off."

I was glad that was the last time. I didn't like being told to fuck off more than three times a night. "That's not going to do it. You're hurting the lady. Let her go now."

We had drawn the attention of Jules' security guy, who was about a half block behind us, as usual. He started making his way towards us, but was cautious. I could see out of the corner of my eye that he was checking everything to ensure this wasn't some type of fabricated distraction. These dudes were pretty good. He was thinking he may need to intervene, but without losing his advantage and coverage. I turned a bit and held up my hand to him. I didn't want to engage this fool, especially in front of Jules and her man, but I also didn't want her security compromised, just in case this was more than it appeared.

"I'm asking you, just please let the lady go, and we can all go in the bar. Drinks on me." A new tactic. Guaranteed to get results.

"He dropped one of her arms and turned to face me directly, slapping his hand heavily on his chest.

"Mother Fucker, do I look like I can't afford my own drinks? You are one step away from getting all my attention, and believe me, you don't want that."

The woman had endured enough, and he was still hurting her. She reached out and scratched at his face, catching his cheek just below his eye. His reaction was to slap her hard, the force jerking her head back. Damn. Out of preservation of my cover, I had waited too long. I moved forward, and he let go of her and took his best swing at me. A roundhouse right. I ducked and moved under his punch, going to my left. His fist glanced harmlessly off the top of my shoulder and his momentum twisted his body left. Now just about behind him, I grabbed his left shoulder with my left hand and slid my right arm around his neck, putting it in a vice in the crook of my arm. Applied some pressure, and he was asleep in five seconds.

I let him down onto the sidewalk, more gently than he deserved, and Jules rushed to the woman. "Are you okay?"

"Yes, yes, I am fine." A local. The moron came to the Country and assaulted a local.

"Do you need for us to take you somewhere. I can get a car here."

"No, no. My friend lives just down the street. I will go there. I will be fine."

"You may want a doctor to check out your jaw. It could be broken." I chimed in.

"It's fine. I'll put some ice on it when I get to my friend's villa."

"You're sure?" asked Jules.

"Yes, yes. Everything is okay."

"Can we call the police?" Jules was trying to be helpful, but I would much prefer not to become known to the local constabulary.

"No. I would rather just go."

"Understood. You better get going. This dude will be waking up in a few minutes and it might be best that none of us are around when he does. I'd hate to have to get into it with him again." Just a little white lie. I would love to get into it with this asshole again.

As the lady walked away, I saw the look from Jules that let me know that I had some 'splainin' to do. Her security guy showed some interest as well. Time for the real estate agent to rationalize exactly how he was able to put some drunk to sleep in five seconds. "I tried wrestling in high school. I wasn't good enough to make the team, but I did learn the sleeper hold." It was weak, but I think Jules bought it. The security dude definitely did not. We may have to get to know each other a little better; something I had avoided. I didn't need them to see me as a threat. Now that this happened, they would have a discussion about me. I may need to nip that. We decided to end our walk and started back towards her condo.

Oh, and some other stuff happened last night. Jules and I made love for the first time. Part of the mission was to befriend her. It's safe to say that we are now, at the very least, friends.

CHAPTER 12

The intelligence was flowing from the Turkish SIC. They tracked Ta to a meeting with an arms dealer in Damascus, and picked up some more chatter about deliveries and payments. Somehow or other, they also got access to the dealer's bank account. After this was all over, they are going to bankrupt him and give the intel and evidence they have to the Lebanese State Security and Interpol. This dude is going to hurt. I may even pay him a visit soon—kind of a pro-bono good deed for humanity.

There was talk about RPGs and mortars. Four total. The Turks know how much money Ta has access to, and based on that info, he blew his wad on the four missiles. That was actually good for a couple of reasons. One, there won't be any surprise munitions unless something financially big happens for Ta, which the Turks would know that right away with the close tabs they keep on him. And two, these missiles have limited range and are not as accurate as their counterparts made by the Americans. Gives me a defined perimeter to work with once I know what the target is.

I still did not know the specifics of the attack, and therefore still had no idea how I was to stop it. Likewise, no idea of how to ensure that Ta gets put in the middle of it. But things had a way of coming together when you're on the right side. So I spared myself the worry and started hunting for clues on my own. I started asking myself the most obvious questions. How will Ta ensure that Jules is exactly where he plans the attack, at the exact right time? Or am I assuming too much? Maybe Ta will wait to find out where she will be at some point and plan the attack around her in real time? That leaves a lot to chance, unless he has no hesitation about harming innocents. Who am I kidding? He's not worried about innocents. And he has to have help-someone has to fire the missiles. Who will that be?

That's a place to start—who will be manning the missiles? Muji has no military. Ta will be close enough to Jules during the attack to rush in and be the late hero, so it won't be him. Who is close to Ta that could be trusted forever with this secret? Or who could he pay to fire the missiles and be sure that it would never come back to him? He wasn't very good at finding an arms dealer—his impatience made him careless and the Turks got the goods on him. Will he be as reckless trying to find a shooter? If so, wouldn't the intel be out there by now? I'm saying yes, it would be out there by now if he had been searching for or hiring a rogue missile guy. So it's someone close to him. Good assumption to start with. I shared my thoughts through the secure network with the SIC and moved on to another question.

The possible locations and times are still stuck in my craw. They will always be dependent on where Jules is. I try to think like Ta. I know that he is lazy, and I know that he is impatient; those traits dominated his arms search, and the deal. If Ta knows of a place and time in advance, that makes his planning much easier, and more likely to succeed. That suits his laziness. Once he has those details secured, he will feel relieved. That quenches his natural impatience. If he is too lazy to orchestrate Jules being in a certain location at a certain time, then he will just wait until he knows one such place and time for sure, and then insert the details into his plan. While this option takes into account his laziness, it doesn't do anything for his impatience. He will be a mess waiting to know exactly when and where his grand plan will kick off. And he would constantly be wondering if he could even find a good opportunity where he could both set the attack in motion and still be close to ground zero, but out of the direct line of fire. And meet those conditions with limited time to set it all up. I settle on the first option being the most likely: He will try to get her to a designated location at a designated time. I send this theory off to the SIC. I could be two-for-two. Or I could be oh-for-two.

I had more to consider. It strikes me that the SIC has gathered lots of information since their initial suspicions generated this mission. Have the Turks cleared the King of suspicion? If so, do they have enough intel to pass on to the King right now and stop this whole deal? Would the King be convinced from what we have that Ta is unfit for the Crown? The threat towards Jules is credible and the evidence points directly to Ta. Would the King accept that and slam Ta? I shared these thoughts with the SIC. If the King was not involved, this was the best solution.

CHAPTER 13

The SIC only kept me waiting about 24 hours. They identified Ta's closest confidant as Mistaf. He had been Ta's assistant his entire adult life. Loyal to a fault, not a genius by any stretch, but keen ambition to work and live in the Palace. And an interest in weaponry. His internet had a trail of web searches on firing RPGs and mortar launchers. Bingo. We know who the trigger man will be. Maybe the King could turn him during interrogation?

They had nothing on the location of the attack. It wasn't talked about on any platforms to their knowledge. Was I wrong about Ta's impatience?

SIC was operating under their own government's radar on this one, therefore they had no official channels with which to get an audience with the King of Muji. They weren't entirely confident that the King was completely innocent in this either. So they were not going official on this. They had strayed too far out of their lane, and unless the risk was the certain loss of Jules, they were not exposing themselves. They presented this as if it would mean the end of the careers for everyone at the SIC that played any part in this.

And they would step away if I said or did anything that would lead to them. I needed them in case I couldn't preempt the attack, and do so very soon—they were my only source of intel. When I took the job, I promised them that their involvement would not be exposed. But like them, all bets are off if necessary to save Jules.

But what about my role? What if I told Jules everything, we go meet with the King, I give him what I have without divulging the involvement of Turkey? Jules may have a feel for whether or not the King is part of this. And if she trusts the King, she could vouch for me, and maybe he would believe my story? He could take Ta's future off the table and Jules would be safe. I would be burned, but that could be fixed. I could never be Buck again, but so what? Small price to pay to save Jules' life and an entire Kingdom from a corrupt future King.

That's it. I'll come clean with Jules and convince her to go to the King, if she trusts him. I have enough of a story, but if the King doesn't believe me—I doubt he'll throw Ta away with just one stranger's story—I'll have to divulge the work of the SIC. The problem with that is the SIC won't back my story. They made that clear. And even if Jules vouches for me, the King would be suspicious that she is influenced by our friendship. I would think about all of these things if I were in his position. The upside is that it would definitely foil Ta's plans for now. The downside is that it's likely not enough for the King to put him out of the picture at the risk of a Royal scandal. And Ta won't stop, so if he has any access at all, Jules' life remains in danger. If he can't get his way now, he will try again in the future. And I won't be there to stop him. So maybe it's a bad idea to tell everything to Jules.

Once again, I find myself wishing for the clean finality of an assassination. Maybe I'll go rogue.

CHAPTER 14
Hours later

I wake up in a sweat, fighting a conscience that has no place in my life. It has become obvious to me that I am worrying too much about details that don't concern me. What did Jane Austen say? Vanity working on a weak mind results in mischief? Something like that. I am a professional operative. Things like trying to influence a King and finding alternative measures so that I won't have to complete my mission are not part of my job. They aren't even part of my character. Things have to be black or white for me. I have a reputation and I hope not to be sniping people when I'm 80 years old. My work, and my eventual retirement, depends on the preservation of my reputation and the completion of jobs as they were commissioned. What, I'm supposed to fall in love with a Princess and be her loyal servant when she ascends to the Throne? Even if she were that serious about me, is that a life that I could ever live? I don't have to think about that very long. It's not. I could not. So the craziness has to stop and I am refocusing on my job.

I temporarily allowed my delusions to detour me from my mission. Vanity working on a weak mind….

No more.

CHAPTER 15

The morning comes with a little softer perspective. The half a bottle of bourbon before bed last night brought me to my emotional knees. It made me uncomfortable for trying to do the right thing. But it also helped me step back and look objectively at what I am doing. Coffee has awakened me and now that the cobwebs and bourbon are out of my system, I know what my path is. I can do the right thing and still protect the integrity of the job.

I can tell Jules what is going on and she can make a decision for herself. If she chooses to go to the King and take her chances with the future, then at least she will be safe for now. And my job will be over. If she doesn't believe me and kicks me out of her life, then I will complete the mission from afar, somehow. I have been through worse.

A message is waiting from the SIC. They still have nothing on a location or time. I'm off to see Jules.

The Princess is especially radiant today. We walk to a favorite breakfast place and load up. They offer a semi American breakfast: eggs, bacon, toast, and the

Greek version of hash browns. I founder myself and feel pretty damn good about it. I eat well when my path is clear. Jules has a croissant and tea and accuses me of flirting with the server. I was guilty, so it was a short conversation

"I need to tell you something".

"What's that, Romeo?"

I give her a look that acknowledges my high school behavior. It's the least she deserves. "First, every feeling I have expressed to you is genuine. Every intimate moment has been real. And this friendship is authentic. No matter what I say from here forward, you must agree that you believe those things."

"You don't know me well, so I will give you a pass on that ridiculous plea. I believe you, and I believe in us. Nothing you can say now would convince me that our time together has not been real. I have lived my life around Royals, which are much the equivalent of politicians in your Country. Essentially, they are liars. Sometimes they are required to lie to protect the citizenry; but nonetheless, they are liars. I learned early in life to be able to separate people's behaviors from their character. Even those with integrity are sometimes forced to be, let's say, less than truthful. I have no illusions that everything you have told me is exactly the truth. You are on holiday in paradise. It would be unusual if you didn't embellish somewhat. But you stay very humble, even though you could tell me anything and I would have no way of disproving it. So here's what I believe. I believe that you are a person of integrity, even if you have lied to me. And if you have,

I will assume there is a good reason for that. I know we're strangers, Buck. But we're strangers in love. So confess your indiscretions if you must, and we'll go on from there."

Wow. She says we're in love. I have to think about that a second, but it hits me with all force that she is right. "We are in love, aren't we? As good as that makes me feel, it won't make this any easier."

"Buck, just go ahead."

"Okay. I'm not exactly who I say I am. But I am not after anything from you. My deception has been about your safety. I was sent to save you. Someone is plotting to kill you. Someone in your family. Your cousin, Ta, has made plans to launch what will appear to be a terrorist attack on Greece while you are here, and you are to be a casualty of that attack. He wants to be the next King and he will do anything to make that happen."

She thought for a minute. She looked pensive, but not surprised. And definitely not scared. What a woman. "Ta has made his feelings known about my place in the lineage. He feels like he was robbed of the chance to be King. And he was. But this type of savagery is not new. The Royal lineage has known this before. Not long ago, when the previous King was still alive, the brother of the direct heir set her up. He framed her for drug smuggling in England. The fact was, she was guilty of her own sins against the Kingdom; she was in bed with Russia. The King was very perceptive and had been suspicious of her. He sniffed out that she was spying, but wanted to avoid the scandal of having a spy in the Royal family. It also gave him a channel to mislead Russia when it served his purpose, so he was content to sit on it for a time. But her brother's corruption rushed the timeline. After the King learned of the drug set up, his intuition told him that there was more to the story. And there was. The brother was only able to set up the Princess because the drug operation was his. The King sent some information to the UK, and when Scotland Yard asked for the brother to be extradited, the King banished him for life. That is the corruption I have lived through. But this—murder and terrorist attacks—this is different, even for someone as devious as Ta. And make no mistake, he is devious. I just never thought he would go this far. So I must ask, do you believe that all of this is true? I mean, how much is speculation and how much is fact?"

So I gave her all the details; even the suspicions about the King. She was bright. She could see that the loopholes were but conveniences to make an argument against the truth; they were not compelling enough for any sort of exoneration of Ta.

"I see", she pondered. "I have some decisions to make."

"Yes, Jules, I'm afraid you do. But please don't take too long. When Ta gets to the island tomorrow, the threat becomes immediate."

CHAPTER 16

She called me and we met in front of the apartment for a walk. In some ways, it seemed so final, like our last walk together forever.

"I know what I must do. My mind is made up. So listen and decide if you want to be a part of it or not. If not, you can leave me with the memory of our time. But I will not change my mind. Agreed?"

"No. But tell me anyway."

"You're a stubborn man. I see why you have never been married."

"Right. So tell me, what do you want to do?"

"I want this to play out. I trust the King, but I suppose there is a very remote possibility that he is involved or maybe has some knowledge. I can't believe for a second that he knows of any plot to kill me—but what if I'm wrong? So for the moment, I'm setting aside the idea of disclosing anything to the King. And whether the King is aware of the plot or not, the way to ensure that Ta is punished is to catch him red-handed in this. There must be no doubt that Ta is behind it. The King would have no choice but to deal with Ta then. So we go forward with your mission as you described it to me yesterday. We foil the plot, save my life, and in the process, expose Ta as the master mind. And trust me when I tell you, that is the most inaccurate use of that term you will ever experience."

The lady had balls. "You're sure? Because this could look kind of crazy. Setting yourself as bait to ensure your ascendency to the Throne? Some might say you are not mentally fit to serve, were they to hear you right now." I was mostly kidding about the mental part. She was just plain brave.

"They will never know. Right now, this is only between you and me. I have not consulted with my aides or my security force. What do you say?"

"I can't let you do this alone. If I do, I won't get paid." That got me a rather forceful punch to the chest.

"You can be such an ass sometimes, you know?"

"I admit nothing."

"So where do we go from here? Do we involve my security force? Do we warn my aides? I do not want them in harms' way, not for a minute."

"We should certainly leave the aides out of it if we know details in advance. We can make sure they stay away. A big "if", I know, but it's all we have. As far as the security guys, do you trust them not to snitch to Ta?"

"I have no reason not to trust any of them."

"Any of them have a connection to Ta?"

"I don't think so."

"Well, if there is some way you can check on that, I would think that would be a good idea."

"Okay. I'll call the head of the security force for the entire Royal Family. He knows everything about these men. And I know he can be trusted."

"Please don't let them in on anything until you get some assurances. We can't risk Ta hearing anything. I mean, if you're really serious about seeing this through."

"I've made up my mind. Get on board, sailor."

"Aye Captain. I think we should go over your itinerary while you're here. We have to assume that Ta already knows it."

"Itinerary? I'm on holiday. I don't have an itinerary."

"Okay. Is there anything that you typically do on holiday? Ta will surely know that. Maybe we can start there."

"Well, really all the stuff you already know. I go to the beach when one is around. I like to go out and listen to music. And sometimes dance. I love eating in out-of-the-way restaurants, you know, the local places. I love walking and exploring. Oh, and boats—I like boats."

"Good start. Keep thinking about that. Have you made any specific plans?"

"Um, yes, a few things. I have an appointment with a stylist in two weeks—can't go too long without that. I'll be getting my nails done the same day. The aides made a couple of dinner reservations—I can give those to you. I think we have planned a wine tour on the mainland. I'm not thinking of anything else right now."

"That's fine. We can talk more. And get with your aides—see what else they may have planned. No surprises. Cool?"

"Sure. I appreciate this, you know. Really. But you need to remember one thing. Ta is NOT going to dictate my life—not here, not in Muji, not anywhere. Okay?"

"I like your style."

CHAPTER 17

Ta elected to fly into Athens and charter a yacht to take him to the island. A big yacht. Over 100'. The trip was official, so the entire expense was on the King's tab. His entourage included Mistaf, two porters, two pages, two aides, and a four-man security force. The aides and the pages were all women who were used to being paid for their special services to men. Ta was known to be a ladies man—he got every woman he ever paid for.

He rendezvoused with the missile transport in open waters, the coordinates sent via secure email and intercepted by the SIC. SIC got plenty of satellite photos of the shipping vessel and the exchange. When the dust cleared, the shipping company would face similar circumstances as the Lebanese arms dealer. Another one bites the dust. The missiles were secured below deck and Mistaf began familiarizing himself with them. Similar enough to the videos. Gave him a little more confidence for his part of the attack. After an hour or so of repetitive practice movements, Mistaf went topside to unwind from the tedium. Ta was standing at the railing, surveying the sea like he was already King. Sad thing, because that sea had nothing to do with Muji. But such are the delusions of madmen.

"Ah, Mistaf. We'll have to look into buying a Royal Yacht when I become King, don't you think?"

"Yes, my Prince. A new yacht. The Caspian will be our domain."

"Mistaf, you do know that the Caspian Sea has no passage to the ocean? A yacht such as this must roam the oceans of the world."

"My apologies, Ta. The seven seas it is. Maybe raise a pirate flag?"

"Mistaf, do you mock me?"

"No my Prince. The fatigue from the relentless training for the launches has muddled my brain. Of course we will sail the oceans. Your Royal Yacht will be known worldwide. The flag of Musjistan will be seen in harbors from California to Barcelona to Japan and everywhere in between."

"Yes. But the wait may be too much for me."

"My Prince?"

"Who knows how long the King may live, left to his own fate? As the direct descendent, my access to him will be unfettered. If something should happen to him to hurry along his demise, well, then so be it, right?"

"Ta, the King has been particularly good to you. He has favored you over his granddaughter at times. You would repay him by shortening his life?"

"Mistaf, the old man has lived his life. It is time for me to live mine. And you, yours. Are you not anxious to take your place as First Advisor to the Crown?"

First Advisor? Mistaf hadn't heard this before. "But of course my Prince. You have not shared this wonderful news with me."

"That's because it will never happen if you fail your mission and screw up the missile launches. That is your test."

Some test, he thought. Fail the test, and First Advisor to the Crown will be the least of his worries. A death sentence will hang over him. But still, First Advisor was nice thought. "I will not fail."

"Good. Now I must prepare to go ashore. Meet me below in a few minutes."

The yacht was anchored about 100 yards off the island—there was no port on the island that could handle a yacht of that size. But it was equipped with a small skiff. A quick boat ride and he could be at any dock on the entire island. Ta didn't want to rely on anyone else for transportation, should anything go south. With a yacht waiting close by for him, he would be self-sufficient in the transportation department if need be.

Before he shuttled to the island, Ta went below and had Mistaf brief him one last time on his new-found expertise with the missiles and launchers, and what type of features a good launching point would require. Mistaf sounded convincing, and Ta bought it. Mistaf had some reservations, though. He wasn't sure he could really fire the missiles in the quick succession needed to mirror a real terrorist attack. But he was determined to continue practicing until he was at least close. After all was done and the Princess was dead, it wouldn't matter anymore. The King would die of old age—or of Ta—and Mistaf would then be moving into the Palace. Not as an aide, but as First Advisor—the second most powerful person in the Kingdom. After the briefing, he retreated to the hold to practice, and would stay there throughout the evening. Ta took the skiff to the island to meet with the Princess and play his part.

CHAPTER 18

"Greetings, cousin! How was your journey?" Jules embraced Ta with the aplomb of a Hollywood Oscar winner. She had elected to meet him at the dock to help support the façade that she was actually happy to see him.

"Delightful, Jules. These waters are amazing." They were both playing their parts, but only one knew the other was full of shit.

"So I see you commissioned a little boat for your trip? Very nice!"

"Yes. You'll have to go out and see her."

"Great. Can't wait. I have a big dinner celebration planned for you tonight. I hope you're hungry?"

"Famished, and looking forward to tasting all the delicacies of this beautiful island."

"You won't be disappointed."

They walked to the cars and made the short trip to Jules condo. Ta acted impressed, although he thought a condo was well below Royalty, but he wanted no bumps in the relationship. Jules had to be completely comfortable with him and trust him. There would be no talk of anyone ascending to the throne; Ta knew that Jules detested those conversations.

Not too far away, I watched. Ta was not an impressive person. He moved and acted like a person due all the privileges of the world. Just the kind of person I detested. And I still wanted to kill him.

Although not positive, my feeling was that his boy Mistaf was not with him. It looked as though only the security force and female companions ventured off the yacht. No problem. I'll get acquainted with him later.

I kept watch until they entered the condo. I wasn't concerned for Jules' safety tonight. The missiles were tucked away on the yacht, according to the SIC. For now, I would have a couple of hours while Jules spun her story and acted gracious to the moron. Time enough for a bourbon and a cigar. There was a place just up the hill, so I took my thoughts and headed there.

CHAPTER 19

Thinking was never my strong suit. I was never known to overintellectualize anything. Always felt like thinking too much meant that you weren't doing anything. I liked to act. Not "act" like the theatre; "Act" like to take action. Meet things on head on. This job has caused me lots of thinking already. Trying to figure out the plan. Trying to follow the morsels of information to some logical conclusions. In some ways, the story of my life.

College was a washout because I never wanted to be there—never enjoyed trying to understand esoteric concepts. So I wasted a pretty nice football scholarship. As a senior in high school I was 6'2', 185, and liked to hit. I was a linebacker and had some success running down a few wide receivers, so it got the attention of a lower-tier D-1 school and they gave me a chance. Universities should turn college athletics into a degree program. I would have graduated—probably. Never cared for school or studying. Thankfully I had good genes that got me through high school. Both my parents were smart. Dad was a country preacher with a master's degree in Divinity. Mom, while never formally educated past high school, was the wisest, smartest person I ever met. But because of their chosen paths—Dad a pastor, Mom the homemaker—I was always the least fortunate kid in my little universe in terms of money and material things. We were dirt poor. But in terms of family and love, I was the richest kid I knew.

After dropping college, the next logical step for the son of a WWII Marine was the military. I enlisted, got promoted a couple of times, and got sent to Warrant Officer School. Ended up running the Criminal Investigative Division on my last post for the United States Army, and was okay with that. When it came time to leave that life behind me, I was recruited by the NSA. They honed the rough edges and took me to my current skill level, then put me on a dark ops team that dominated my time during the last six years in the agency. Left that racket under a cloud, because I can't take orders from traitors—another story, another time—and started doing private work. Who knew there was a market for this stuff? I stick to working only for the good guys, although I have been fooled once or twice. In this case, I think the SIC are pretty good guys; they just got hold of information that they really can't capitalize on themselves. Thankfully they had conscience enough not to sit on it.

The cigar is short and the glass is empty, although refilled once. My thoughts have struck a sentimental note, so I sit here for just a bit longer, and ponder the days to come. Jules must be safe. The attack must be stopped. Ta must be assigned the blame for all of it. Those are the things that have to happen. That's what needs to stay central in my mind until this is over.

CHAPTER 20

Jules' call was a surprise. We didn't plan on communicating directly too much while Ta was around. But she had some good info.

"The First Advisor to the King called me last evening and gave me a few official appearances to make while I'm here. He says that I need to start conducting some duties on behalf of the Crown."

"Okay. And they are?"

"He asked me to meet with the Council of the Isles next week. They are meeting on the next island to the east. I'm to tell them that the King is planning to build a holiday retreat here and wants their input about the best locations on the islands. Then he asked me to represent him at the Coronation of the new Greek Cardinal later this week. That's this Friday. He also wants me to attend the opening of the Russian opera troupe in Athens. It is next weekend. The Grecian First Lady will be in attendance. I will be her guest—she has given me a private loge."

"That it?"

"That's all he told me about last night."

"And does Ta know about all this?"

"Yes. He is to accompany me to all of them."

"Alright. Well, like every other great operative, I don't believe in coincidences. These events could be an assist for Ta's planning. How much of this would Ta have known about before he came down here?"

"I don't know. But the King doesn't usually share much outside of his close circle."

"Doesn't really matter. Ta knows now. We have to consider these events targets of opportunity for him."

"So what now?"

"Depends. Will you consider skipping everything and just going home?"

"I will not. We are past that, and you know it. Besides, if I know Ta, and I do, he will be suspicious if I leave. He'll go forward with an attack just to deflect blame from him."

"He'd kill people just to prove he wasn't planning to kill you?"

"I have no doubt. If his plan gets exposed, and an attack occurred anyway, it will look like we got bad information—like Ta was being set up. I mean, if I wasn't there to be killed, why would there have been an attack at all? If nothing else, it would make it more difficult to convince the King." She paused, and I could hear her angst. "But all of that doesn't matter to me now. What matters is that we stop the attack. And I need you to make sure we do that."

"You don't have to worry about that. Can we talk about your security force?"

"Sure. What about them?"

"Have you made the inquiry about them?"

"Yes, last night. All of them have worked with Ta at one time or another, mostly when special events require more security. According to their boss, no one likes working around Ta. He is demanding and condescending. That's all he could give me, other than his assurances that he only hires trustworthy people."

"That doesn't convince me. No matter what the details of the attack, we need at least one other person that we can trust. Someone has to be with you and someone has to sabotage the missile launches. I'm all we have for stopping the launches. We have to be confident that your security team will protect you while I'm doing that."

"I think that even if they hated me, they would have no loyalty to Ta. You see, all security forces would be replaced if Ta became King. The contract would go to the person that gave Ta the biggest kickback—all of his contracts are awarded that way. These guys would be out of a job, and they know it."

"So, bottom line, you trust them to keep you safe?"

"Yes. I do. In fact, I'll go one step farther. The more I think about it, the more I believe they would kill Ta and take their chances with the King before they will allow me to be put in danger."

"Really?"

"Yes, really."

"That makes me a little more comfortable. Kinda been wanting to kill him myself." Oops. Too far.

"No one has to die, right? We can do this and everyone can survive."

"That's an honorable objective, and if we foil the rocket launches, then right, no one probably dies. But if I think anything is putting you in danger, I'm alerting your security team and you will be taken wherever they have to take you to keep you safe. No argument. Agreed?"

"No. But go on."

"Smartass."

"How does it feel? Dish it, but can't take it?"

"Something like that."

CHAPTER 21

Recon is a methodical process that can twist without notice. You work a pattern, and then run across an anomaly, and have to start the pattern all over again. And then you hit another bump, and start all over again. Real work. But an absolute necessity in a business that cannot afford surprises. Operations tend to go sideways when unexpected things happen. Recon is about giving you every chance to control the outcome of your operation. And I had a lot of it to do in the next few days.

I have to recon all of the planned events, and when necessary, divert my attention to recon more immediate unplanned events as they come up. Today, the cathedral. I dress as absolutely plain as I can. I take a generic ball cap and cheap sunglasses. Wearing a reversible T-shirt. As I move around throughout the day, I'll change my look here and there. Hat on, sunglasses off, t-shirt one color, later the other; sunglasses on, hat off, switch the t-shirt, etc. You get the picture. Since I would be spending so much time in the same areas, I needed to try to change my appearance often enough to maybe avoid suspicion from the casual observer. I bring my phone, Leatherman—call me old school—and Glock. One extra mag.

After a call to check in with Jules, I start my day on the roof of a building about a tenth of a mile from the cathedral where the Coronation will occur. The actual Coronation will occur in the sanctuary. Ta can't successfully attack during the ceremony because of the high roof of the sanctuary. It is a tall dome with many beams. When the missiles hit the roof, there would be no control as to where the damage will occur. The reception was to be held in the meeting hall; a low-ceiling extension built off the sanctuary to the south. The location of the meeting hall lent itself to rocket attacks from the west, east and south. The north approach would not be feasible or effective; the missile would have to go through the sanctuary to impact the meeting hall. And the RPGs are not accurate unless there is line-of-sight from the firing point to the target.

My vantage point gives me a view of all but two access routes to the cathedral. One is an alley that leads from the rear door of the cathedral, down a hill, and then turns east to join a road that I can see clearly. The other is a walkway that begins at the same rear door and leads down over the hill, through a small field and winds around into the neighborhood below. After my time on this roof, I will relocate to another perch and watch those back routes for a while. I wait and watch, looking for anything suspicious, for about 45 minutes. I then move to another location and watch the two rear access points for another 30 minutes. Nothing.

The access routes show no suspicious traffic or movement. I walk down and began to work outward from the cathedral, step by step, circling slowly. It's difficult to blend in, but there is really no other way when I'm flying solo. The good news is that the RPGs and mortars have a limited range for the type of pinpoint accuracy Ta needs. A mile would be a stretch for a mortar; and an RPG wouldn't be accurate beyond 300 yards. So there would be no use for the shooter to fire from more than 300 yards away. Even though the mortars could be accurate from farther, the RPGs could not; no way for Mistaf to simulate a single attack if he moved from one firing point to another. And two waves of attack bring much more into the equation—there is simply no upside for Ta. And Ta needs all four to make the impact he wants. I'm hoping that the intel is correct—Ta has only Mistaf to help; but I'm preparing as if has more. So I will recon hard within the 300 yard radius—but will check out the obvious points of launch within a one mile perimeter.

After the first hour, I have not seen anything that would lend cover to a surreptitious mortar launch. Only yards away from the cathedral at this point, I didn't expect the launching to be this close anyway. The mortar tube can be muffled and padded to decrease range, but the distance to impact must allow for the trajectory. Still, I must check every possibility. I decide to stop for tea, just to give the area a break from my presence, and head to a taverna a half a block away. From here, I can still see the front of the cathedral. As I'm rising from my chair to get back to it, a rented pickup rolls by the café and slows in front of the cathedral. I know it's a rental because of the license plate—Greece has special plates for rental cars. I cannot see the occupant, but I can tell that there is only one. I have no vehicle to follow with, so I hustle out of the taverna and climb back up to my first perch. I think I catch a glimpse of the truck to the west, but can't be sure. I wait and watch, again, for another several minutes. I make a mental note of the truck: late model red Silverado, club cab, white camper top, quarter ton. I send a secure email with this info to SIC; they will have the rental contract information in no time. The bad guys may be scouting out their launching location. If that was what was happening, it means that they are not well prepared. That plays to our advantage. Nothing more to see up here, so I go back down and pick up where I left off.

150 yards from the cathedral, I come across an abandoned building—there aren't many of those here—with the roof burned off. It was a garage of some sort in better days. Now it has possibilities as a mortar launching pad. I check it out carefully. While easy to access on foot because of the damaged walk-through door, the main garage door was intact. Inside, there was room for a vehicle—move some debris out of the way, and it would be an easy fit. There is line-of-sight for an RPG launch, as well, if the shooter stands on something to elevate his position. This was a good option.

175 yards to the east of the cathedral was an open field, raised from the main road, but accessible by a path from the berm. A four-wheeler could get up the

path, but other than something like that, you could only make it on foot. Because it was raised from the road, the missiles could be launched from there with relative anonymity. While not quite ideal in terms of line-of-sight, it was still possible. It would all depend if someone was in the area to witness the launch, and how close they were to the field. That lack of cover was a liability for this spot, for sure. After all, it would be a broad-daylight launch.

300 yards to the east was another prospective launching site. An empty house, probably a seasonal place owned by some big money dilbert, with a back lot surrounded by a six foot stone wall. A vehicle could access the lot through a gate at the side of the house, probably there for mower access. Very uncommon on the islands. But workable for a missile launch, and the line-of-sight was adequate for the RPG.

I have gone well beyond the accurate range of the RPG. I spend the next two hours working out to the one mile range. I'm not as meticulous, but note the best options to both facilitate and cover mortar launches. I don't feel great about this part—not as ideally thorough as it should be—but time is short and there is only me.

Now I start working my way back, looking for escape routes to the coast. The shooter will depart Greece with Ta—that's how he got here. Mistaf returning separately from Ta would not look good and be hard to explain. And from what I have learned about this Mistaf character, he couldn't survive alone for very long. He'll want to fire the missiles and make for the yacht like the outgoing tide.

CHAPTER 22

There are four routes that lead down the hill to the coast. Two of them come together just west of the docks; the other two come in from the east. The skiff is at the dock now. Ta went back to the yacht last night, but came back to the island this morning to join Jules for lunch. I suspect that Mistaf made the trip with him. I will check with Jules to see if Mistaf was at lunch.

I get lucky with the exit routes. From the cathedral area, the two roads on the east are the only feasible routes. They work their way down the from the cathedral area in a relatively direct manner. The other two are circuitous routes that would take much longer. Just wouldn't make sense. Even to Mistaf.

The SIC got back to me about the rental truck. Mistaf rented it yesterday afternoon for two weeks, long enough to be available for everything Jules had on her schedule. With the system of ferries it could be taken to the other island and the mainland as well, so I couldn't discount it for any of the events on Jules' schedule. Ta can alibi the rental with the fact that they need transportation while on the island. So it isn't really evidence of his involvement in anything sinister. Yet.

As dusk draws near, I decide to find the truck and check it out. It has to be somewhere on the island. But I'm hungry, and a bourbon or two wouldn't be too bad either.

I decide on another taverna close to the cathedral. A little touristy for my taste, but I've been there before and know the fish will be good. The dining room is big for this island, supporting my theory that the place is more designed for tourists than locals. They even have a hostess, something out of the ordinary for tavernas on the island. She is a Greek beauty, as so many of them are here, and permits me to choose a table near the back, but facing the entrance and the big plate glass window in the front—another unusual feature for the island tavernas.

I order my bourbon and the fish special, a nice one with the head still on, and a light breadcrumb topping. Just as the food is put on my table, three guys coming in the front catch my eye. I've seen one of them before. It doesn't look like a chance encounter, either, as he scans the room until his gaze finds me and stops. It's the drunk woman-beater who I treated to a nap a few nights ago, and he looks to be on a mission. And he brought friends. Huh. The three stooges. They come my way. I don't need this. I have work to do.

Drunk boy steps right up to the edge of my table, clearly demanding attention. But I have none for him. The fish is really good tonight and is taking up all the attention I have to spare. Curley and Mo spread to my right and left. They appear to be local hooligans. They need both a shave and a bath. They're bringing the atmosphere down. None of them have any bulges in their clothing that would suggest they are carrying.

"Hey." What is it with these dudes and their monotonous dialogue? Of course, I ignore him. Taking the high road.

"Remember me?" Still not compelled to give him an audience.

"Fuckface, you listening?" Name calling. Tsk tsk. "You want to do this in here? Cuz we can." Time to humor him I suppose.

"Do what? You came to seek revenge because I stopped you from going to jail the other night?" Maybe I can reason with him.

"I would never go to jail on this island. I own half of it." Now, I knew that was an exaggeration. Should I call him on his lie?

"Look, I'm minding my own business, dining rather peacefully up til now, enjoying this meal and the ambience. If you would like to join me, fine. But otherwise, I'm going to have to ask you to leave me to it. Okay?"

"Why don't we just go outside and see how tough you are when I'm sober." A challenge. How cute. His boys had moved closer, and well within reach. God, I hope we don't have to do this in here.

"I have no desire to go outside and do anything with you—nothing personal. How about this: You have scared me sufficiently and if I ever come across you abusing a young woman again, I promise to let her beat you up herself. Okay? Are we good?"

"We are pretty fucking far from good." Nice line. Wish I would have thought of that one. "Get your ass out of that chair and get outside, or take your beating here. It's going to happen, one way or the other. Doesn't matter where to me." I am completely adverse to making a scene in this taverna, and even more adverse to breaking up the place. But he is starting to get loud. Out of fairness, I think he should know my feelings.

"Let me get this straight. You're willing to make a scene here, bust up this café, and ruin dinner for all these nice people? Is that what you're saying? Because if so, I vote against it. In fact, I refuse to be a part of it. So why don't we meet up in a couple of days and have a fishing contest. You know, first fish, biggest fish, whatever you prefer. Or maybe a chess match? I'm sure we can settle your grievance like gentlemen. You see, I'm eating, and I'm really busy this evening, and I am not going to ruin everybody's meal here just to humor you." I slipped another bite of the fish in my mouth. I have not looked up at him yet. Just don't feel like it.

"No more bullshit asshole. Last chance. You're going outside right now or we take care of you here." He was too loud now. Everybody was gawking. Nobody was enjoying their meals anymore. And he was leaning over the table violating my space. Damn. He was going to make me do it.

"Well, if it's the last chance, I'd hate to miss it." I knock back the rest of my bourbon, took my napkin from my lap and laid it neatly on the table. No reason to act like a Neanderthal just because he is. The server came with the check, likely fearing it wouldn't get paid. "I'll catch you in a couple of minutes, friend. I have to run outside real quick." I get up and walk easily through the café, smiling and nodding to the patrons so as to maybe relieve some of the tension that dickhead had caused.

Once out the door, I walk quickly to my right, and slip into the alley beside the café. I don't need anyone watching this. I am a little ahead of the three stooges so I take another stab at talking them down, although at this point, I don't think I really wanted to talk them out of it. But I turn and face them. "I know you think that this is a good move for you—regain some face, show your boys that nobody gets away with disrespecting you. I get that. So, I give up. You win. You've taught me a lesson and I'll never mess with you again. Cool? And besides, there's only three of you. It's not really a fair fight." I just couldn't help myself. Had to keep going when I could've just shut up.

Curley and Mo come to grab my arms. They are both bigger than me, and I think that was intentional on the part of drunk boy. Fully expecting me to be restrained in short order, drunk boy moves in to start the punishment. But he is too late.

Curley doesn't quite make it to me. He has to go down as soon as I pop his knee clean out of joint with my right foot. That knee will not hold weight again tonight. That leaves poor Mo to endure the hardest body shot I can deliver. I hear his ribs crunch; probably got two of them. Of course, he has to stop his attack to grab his midsection and search for breath. I give him an elbow to the exposed chin, and he is out. By now, drunk boy has started his swing. Didn't we go through this once before? De ja Vue I guess. I reach up and catch his fist in my hand. This is the instant where he realizes that, once more in his pathetic life, he has let his mouth completely override his ass. He can't seem to take the pressure I am putting on his hand, and goes to his knees as the bones crack, leaving me an inviting target. I oblige with another right hand. He's asleep again, but endured so much more to get there than the first time.

Curley begs me not to finish him, and I'm a big softie, so I leave him to his crutch-laden future and go back in to finish that delightful fish.

CHAPTER 23

After paying the check, I head out to start the search for Mistaf's rental. I figure the dock area would be a likely spot, so I head down the hill. Curley is nowhere to be found. Two other stooges appear to be sleeping in the alley.

Walking around the waterfront, I check all the parking lots and driveways. Soon enough, I spot the red Silverado in the far edge of a beach parking area. Public parking. Ta must have run out of the King's money. No one is around, so I decide to take a look. I peek in the cab. Seats, steering wheel, gear shift. All stuff that is supposed to be there. The camper shell door is locked. I pull out my Leatherman and find the right application to pick this rudimentary lock. Haven't picked a lock in a few months, but it's like riding a bike. I take nearly two minutes to open it. Wow. I'm more out of practice than I realized.

The truck bed has a few interesting items. There's a tarp, a six foot step ladder, a new gas can filled with fuel, and binos. Hmm. Everything needed to conceal, aim, and fire a mortar and RPG, and then destroy the evidence. But their ignorance is almost refreshing: A gas fire will not burn hot enough to destroy either the RPG launcher or the mortar tube. Mistaf will leave evidence. And that's a good thing because it's another component of the case against Ta; a bad thing because if we have to rely on burned up mortar tubes and RPG launchers for evidence, it means the rockets were launched. I take several pictures with my phone and keep moving. There is no doubt that the actual munitions are on the yacht. The last part of my recon tonight will involve a long moonlight swim.

I find a place near the docks that provides some foliage to cover what I leave on shore. I take my Leatherman, silenced Glock, and phone. No extra magazine. Worst case scenario, I'll take the gun from the first person I shoot. It will be just like having an extra magazine, but without the weight to swim with. I stash my shoes, shirt, and sunglasses in the foliage. If found, they tell no story. I wrap the mag in my hat and bury it nearby.

The water is calm and the swim is easy enough. Takes me about 10 minutes. Not a good race time—a slow stealth time. Good thing about a yacht—you can climb right out of the water onto the swimmer's deck. After checking to see where the security guys were, I did just that. They were in the pilot house, keeping close watch of basically nothing. I don't want to disturb them, so I sneak down below at the first opportunity. I wondered around a bit, getting the layout. I had done what I could to get an interior layout of the yacht from the web, but the brand was from a specialized builder, so there was no definitive floorplan available.

I find the hold. It is padlocked, and I pick the lock and ease the hatch open. There is a tarp covering something, and I lift it to reveal what I already knew was there. As soon as I see the munitions, I hear someone coming. If I'm caught here, there is no attack and Jules will be safe for now. But Ta will have the rest of his life to change that. Unless maybe I just kill him now…

Can't do it. I promised Jules we would play this her way until and unless her life was in imminent danger. She won't back away from it. If all goes well, this whole episode will someday define her legacy: The courageous Princess who risked her life to expose corruption in the lineage. What a woman. So I quickly replace the padlock and move down the passageway. It's one of the security guys, and he takes up post in front of the hold. I caught him on break. My best plan was to disable the munitions tonight, and leave Mistaf nothing to live fire but his dick when the time came. Having no fear then of an actual launch, I would film him in the act, and then coerce him into telling me everything. Snitching on Ta may be the only way to convince the King to spare his worthless life. His testimony corroborates all the evidence. If he takes the rap himself, he suffers a prolonged painful torturous death at the hands of the King's finest henchmen. If he rats out Ta, maybe the King exiles him, but he lives. My money was on the rat part.

I listen for a few minutes to ensure that the door guard is alone. Hearing nothing, I make my way back up a rear stairwell and onto the lower deck. Nobody around. A security guy still up in the pilot house. I slip down into the water and make my way to shore. Grab my clothes and shoes, dig up the mag, and start the walk up the hill. I have a random thought about three guys showing up at the local urgent care this evening: Two broken jaws, two broken ribs, a dismantled knee, and a broken hand. My apologies to the on-call physician.

CHAPTER 24

Cabernet in hand, I was looking at yet another perfect Greek Isle night from the little balcony off my apartment. I had showered and changed for the occasion. I think about the coronation tomorrow. This could be the one. If the attack is on for tomorrow, I'm prepared. I've put in the work. I've done the recon. I've seen the weapons. I'll stop the attack and Jules will be safe. Sewing up Ta as the bad guy was still not guaranteed. But it will come.

I consider what I have that implicates Ta. The intercepted communications courtesy of Turk SIC. The arms purchase. The money transfer. The munitions transfer. Mistaf's web-based training footprints. The pictures from the pickup bed. Unfortunately I didn't have time to take pictures of the weapons in the yacht hold. But I may have another chance to get them on film later. Especially if nothing happens tomorrow. We'll see.

All in all, it didn't sound like a terrible case. But the King would want it to be conclusive. Solid. Not a chance for other stories to be told that would make things look like coincidence. I can't imagine what kind of story would do that. So I think about that for a while after I top off my wine.

Ta could say that the arms communications were coming from a diverted source, and made to look like they were coming from him. I don't have the confidence that SIC will confirm that beyond what they already have. I expect them to drop off the radar after the attack—or after it's thwarted—and build their case for plausible deniability.

Ta's part of the arms purchase involves a documented trip to Damascus. He could have gone to Damascus for any number of reasons. He likes Lebanese women (who doesn't) and could explain that away as a horny pleasure trip.

The money is a problem for Ta. He spent just about everything he had on the munitions. The wire transfers will show his money going to the dark bank website of the arms dealer. If it was me, I would say that someone hacked my account and moved 200,000 Euros to who knows where. It happens all the time.

The satellite photos show something being moved from a merchant vessel to the yacht that Ta leased. The transfer is corroborated by the meeting in Lebanon and the money transfer. If the meeting and money transfer are discredited, then maybe Ta smuggled some artwork out of Russia, or something else from somewhere else. He could easily come up with some type of contraband to justify a surreptitious transfer from a merchant ship.

Mistaf's training video footprints? Just a coincidence. He is a weapons guy. He's always on the web looking at different guns and munitions. Sadly, that can likely be confirmed, if what I was told about him is true.

The pictures from the truck bed prove nothing except that there were some items in the bed of the Mistaf's rental. They'll say they were there when he rented the truck—he knew nothing about the stuff. Some fool left them when he turned in the rental. Nothing can prove otherwise. Oh, the inventory on the vehicle when he picked it up? Some pimple-faced teenager trying to get done for the day. Just a careless omission by a kid.

Is there any way possible that the King is gullible enough to buy some series of wild stories? These or others? If he fears the scandal, he can use whatever excuse he wants to avoid it. As long as he didn't personally watch Ta shoot a missile at Jules, he could rationalize everything away if he wanted. Let's hope he doesn't want to.

More wine.

CHAPTER 25

The morning is a typical here: Bright sun, nice lazy breeze, cloudless skies, and pristine waters. The day of the coronation. I pour my third cup of coffee, trying to reverse the effects of a sleepless night. This morning, I will take a walk to check the likely launch areas. Then, a visit to the cathedral. A big event like this will mean that people will be there working. I call Jules. She sounds good.

"Hey. Good morning."

"Good morning."

"You okay?"

"Fine. Except my new boyfriend hasn't been around for a few days."

"We knew what this would be like once Ta got in town. No reason for him to know anything about me. You said you wanted to see it through. If he knows about me, he may get suspicious."

"I know. We don't need to re-hash it. Just wanted you to know that I miss you."

"Very sweet. Caught me by surprise. Usually you get right to the point."

I could almost hear her smile. "Yes. And the point is, I miss you."

"Miss you too. After this is over, we'll spend some time, get reacquainted."

"After this is over, you're going to leave. You don't think I know what the deal is?"

That gave me pause. I wasn't ready to think about that yet. "I'd rather save this conversation until Ta is locked up somewhere. I have some friends that can detain him and deliver him to the King after we expose him and his plot."

"I think I can handle that part. I'm a Crown Princess after all. Did you forget?" Flexing her muscle. I like it.

"Never. So you handle it Princess."

"You think we could sneak out for breakfast? I don't expect Ta until around noon. The Coronation isn't until 1."

"You have no idea how much I would enjoy that, but duty calls. I still have lots to do before the ceremony."

"You're boring me."

"Yep. It's a gift. See you soon."

"Okay. And, I want to tell you, you know, in case something happens…"

"No, no. We're not going down that road. You said it best a few days ago. You believe in us. That's all that has to be said. Now go put on your best "I can actually stomach Ta" face and let's get this done."

"Bossy today, are we? I think I kind of like that."

"Don't get used to it. Nobody bosses a queen. Take care, okay?"

"Sure thing. Be careful." We clicked off. I gathered my usual and headed out.

CHAPTER 26

The roads were empty. The island called a holiday for the Coronation. If today was the day for him, that uncomplicated some things for Mistaf. He could maybe get to his spot undetected, and his getaway would be smoother—no traffic and all the cops would be up around the cathedral. All four of them assigned to the island. The mainland considered this a friendly community event, and decided not to send help. Not sure why they didn't see it as a National event; the Cardinal was going to serve the entire Country. I suspect the fact that attendance was by invitation only had something to do with it.

I have been through the scenarios time and again, and the one stump I keep sawing into is Mistaf. There is no indication that he will have help. No intelligence, no evidence, nothing. But I have wondered all along if maybe there was someone else we don't know about that could have been brought in on the secret? Jules says that Ta trusts no one but Mistaf. Mistaf has done the training on his personal computer. Every computer in Ta's residence had been tracked for weeks by the

Turks, without any indication of munitions or weapons of any kind. But it still bothers me, so I am leaving myself plenty of time before the reception to hopefully overcome any unforeseen eventualities.

The likely ambush points are just the way they were when I scouted them yesterday. I believe the two spots uphill are the most likely, but if it were me, that is exactly why I wouldn't use them. Mistaf has no operational history, but maybe he reads spy novels. Doesn't matter. If he lands anywhere around here today, I'll find him.

I enter the meeting hall at the cathedral. Several nuns are scurrying around, covering tables, wrapping silverware, putting out dishes. A man and woman were cleaning; he on the floors, her on the windows. I suspect this has all been scrubbed recently, and they are touching up. This is big for the Parish; they had likely been prepping for weeks.

I approach one of the younger nuns. "Good morning."

"Hello. Can I help you?"

"I'm on holiday on the island and I heard about the Coronation. Thought I would stop by and see when it starts."

"It starts at 1 p.m. today, but I'm afraid you need an invitation."

"Oh. Well, could you invite me?" I flashed a smile.

She smiled too, but it was that contradictory soft, deadly smile that only nuns can summon. "Someone much more important than me must tender that invitation."

"You mean God?"

Now she smiles for real. "No. Just the retiring Cardinal. He is in charge."

"The Cardinal for all of Greece? I fear he left me off the list." She looked like she might be done with all this fun, but I pressed on. "So, looks like there will be a big meal."

"No. Just some snacks. Hors d'oeuvres, little sandwiches, finger foods of lamb and goat, that sort of thing." Ugh. That beautiful ocean full of tasty whitefish less than a mile away, and they're serving goat.

"And lots of wine."

"Yes, the Cardinal does like his wine." Cute. She can joke about her boss. Well, at least her earthly boss.

"I'm ashamed to say, but I have never been to one of these my entire Catholic life," A white lie to a nun. Where will it end? "Will they have a big ceremony or what?"

"Most of us have never been to one of these. Your Catechistic vows are safe." A better smile. She was on fire. "The attendees will assemble in the sanctuary first. The Cardinals will enter in a grand procession. Leading the procession will be the retiring Cardinal, followed by the new Cardinal, and then all the visiting Cardinals."

"Wow. That sounds like a lot of Deity."

"It is. We've never had any Cardinals visit us, except Cardinal Veche. He's the retiring Cardinal."

"So your Priest—will he run the ceremony?"

She smiled again. "Father Andino will be in the congregation, with the rest of the invited guests."

"Knocked right out of his pulpit, huh?"

"So to speak. But he's a modest person. I expect he will enjoy seeing things from that viewpoint for a change."

"Good for him. Um, would it be a great inconvenience if I were to ask to use your restroom."

"Of course not. Everyone has to at one point or another." I landed the Seinfeld of nuns. "Right through that door way, to your right just before you enter the sanctuary."

"Thanks."

I strolled down the hall like I belonged there and went into the sanctuary. All was as reported. The high domed ceiling would preclude any attack here. Maybe the RPG through the windows, but the mortars were rendered useless here. They had to land on the place. They couldn't be shot through a wall with any effective kill radius. Pretty much only those folks by the wall would get hurt.

The hallway I went through was one of two that led from the sanctuary to the meeting hall. The hall in front was more suited for those on the dais; the rear one was much wider. This is the hallway that Jules would walk through to get to the reception. The meeting hall was completely open; one room, no dividing walls. With any luck, the low ceiling would be as intact tomorrow as it is right now. A direct hit with a mortar would put everyone in the room in danger. If you add another mortar and a couple of RPGs to the mix, it was mass death. An awful feeling swept over me. Jules is trusting me to stop the attack; trusting me completely. I am used to being trusted as a professional. But as a friend? This is something new. I didn't like it. Not at all.

CHAPTER 27

I wanted a little reassurance, so I left the hall and called Jules. "Are you doing okay?"

"I am. Why? Is there a problem?"

"You mean other than Ta wanting to kill you and anybody that happens to be around you when he does?"

She wasn't having any of that drama. "C'mon. You know what I mean."

"I'm asking you again. Please don't go through with this. Don't go to the Coronation. Don't go to the Council meeting. Don't go to the opera. Too many innocent lives at risk."

"We've been over this, Buck. Ta will attack somewhere, with or without me around. If I balk at attendance at any one of these events, he'll know something is afoot, and he'll launch the attack just to prove they weren't aimed at me. Listen, you will stop the attack before it happens. You can do this. You will do this. You know I trust you, right?"

"Yes. You trust me too much. These people don't have to be risked."

"They won't be. If things fall apart, I'll sound the alarm. I'd warn everybody at every event before I would risk their safety."

"You want to be known as the Princess who cried wolf? What a way to start your reign."

"I won't be known as anything. Nobody here knows who I am."

"You make it hard to love you, you know that?"

"No, I don't know that. I don't think anyone has ever tried before." That was quite a revelation. Calmed me down a bit.

"Well, here's the deal. If this all goes south, and I can't stop an attack, I'm kidnapping you and probably shooting Ta."

"You can kidnap me any time. But we're trying to get out of this without losing lives, remember? Isn't that why I got this panicked call?"

"I said innocent lives…"

"Touché. Are we agreed?"

"No. But I'll go along. See you soon."

CHAPTER 28

Moving from one location to another, I began to wonder how early Mistaf would set up if this was his big day. He wouldn't want to wait until too late, in case he ran into some complication and couldn't get the missiles launched. Any wrinkle could mess up his plan. Even he was smart enough to realize that.

I was still concentrating on the two uphill locations and keeping my eyes peeled for the truck. At noon, I noticed some activity in the walled-in back lot I had scouted. Just a flash of movement. I was not close enough to tell what it was, so I worked my way toward the house. I got to the front and edged down the side of the house—the side without the gate. As I started to peek around the corner, I heard voices. Great. More than one person. I slowly looked. There were more than two people. There were three. Teenagers, smoking a joint. I got out of there and went to check my other potential firing spot.

A few minutes later, and I was outside of the burned out garage. The big door looked different. I had memorized the position of everything, and it was off, just a touch. I went closer and saw that the twig I wedged in the door frame was lying on the ground. I moved around the building to the walk-through door. I knew I would be able to see through the damaged frame. The red Silverado was there. The camper shell had been removed, and the step ladder was set up in the bed. That would give the RPG a clear line of sight to the meeting hall. Sitting on the tailgate, biting his nails, was a scumbag that looked amazingly like the pictures of Mistaf I had studied. So the coronation it was.

Mistaf was going to hear me if I busted down the door. But he wouldn't hear the shot from my silenced Glock. I knew this was the decision I would likely have to make in this situation: Just shoot him and get it over, or try to capture him and get him to talk. I had promised myself that I would only go the capture route if I was certain that no lives would be risked. He was not holding a weapon. I couldn't see in the truck bed, but I figured the munitions were there. If I came in hard, he would not have a chance to get to the munitions. So I did. And he didn't. He froze, which was good, because I wasn't adverse to shooting him to start with. The RPGs were laying in the truck bed, locked and loaded. I told him to keep quiet and grabbed his phone off the tailgate. I pulled out my trusty duct tape and secured him and his mouth. I disengaged the rockets from the launchers and stomped the launchers into pieces. I grabbed his taped wrists and dragged him with me as I searched for the mortars. I checked the cab first. They weren't there. I searched the garage, which took no time because it was basically rubble. No mortars. This is not good. I held the gun to his eye, with enough force to send a message about how serious I was.

"The mortars. Where are they?" He shook his head. No way this shithead was playing tough guy with me. I gave him a good slap on the side of the head with the Glock.

"I'm taking the tape off of your mouth. When I do, you will tell me where the mortars are. And you will do that immediately. Otherwise, you will limp the rest of your life. Got it?" He nodded.

I ripped the tape off his mouth. His first words were "I don't know what you're talking about." So I put my hand over his mouth and shot him through the right knee. He acted like he felt it.

His screams were muffled by my hand and therefore not loud. But annoying. "Stop screaming. You sound like a little bitch." I gave him a few seconds to get composed. "Now when I take my hand off your mouth, you will immediately tell me where the mortars are. I'll even start the sentence for you, so all you have to say is the exact location. Otherwise, you'll leave here without a leg to stand on. Got it?" He nodded. "Okay. Here we go. The mortars are…." I took my hand away.

"The bottom of the road, a half a click, on the roof of a hotel under a tarp."

"Good. Now who is there with them?"

"One of Ta's security force."

"Does he know how to fire a mortar?"

"Yes. He was trained by the Russians."

"Is he alone?"

"Yes. Yes."

"Are there any more munitions anywhere."

"No. That's all. The mortars are everything."

"I'm coming back here, and If you've lied to me, I'll cut off your ears, then cut out your eyes, and then cut off your fingers. I'll drag it out for hours. Now, is what you told me the entire and exact truth?"

"Yes."

I taped his mouth up again and quickly secured him to a beam with more tape. Then wrapped a couple of lengths of it around his wound. You gotta love duct tape. I threw open the garage door, got in the truck, and backed out. Got out, shut the garage door, and headed down the road. I knew the hotel he was talking about. Had reconned it as part of the potential mortar perimeter. Rounding the first curve going down the hill, I could see the roof of the hotel, and what appeared to be a tarp thrown over a wire. If this guy was trained by the Russians, he would be able to pinpoint the zone. Under no circumstances could I let him get a mortar away.

CHAPTER 29

I pull up in front of the hotel. 12:30. Still plenty of time. I make my way up the front stairwell. During my recon, I discovered that the back stairwell was mostly used to store old furniture and was damn near impassable. Somebody needed to call the fire marshal. The four flights of stairs behind me, I slowly push on the door. It's not locked. It's blocked. I push, keeping the momentum down and the force up. I can't forecast my presence too early and risk him taking a pot shot at the cathedral. The door begins to move, and whatever is blocking it was not making much noise as it gives. I just need a foot or so gap to squeeze through. Almost there. A little more. And there. I push my head through and see the back of the makeshift tent. No sign of movement. I check my flanks and squeeze through the opening. I step out onto the rubberized roofing—that's why my forced entry was so silent. No movement yet. I creep up to the tent and find an opening. I peer into it. The mortar launcher and both shells are there. But no security guy. The launcher seems to be already targeted. I go under the tarp and grab the launcher. I break the legs off and look out. He has to be here somewhere. As I search behind the air conditioning units, the security guy exits the back stairwell, unbeknownst to me. The door is propped open, so I hear nothing. He sees me immediately and, having the tactical advantage, decides to draw his weapon. I hear it clear the holster. Just barely, but it is a sound I will always recognize—not really a click, not really a swish. Some combination. But distinguishable from all other sounds in the world. My drop and turn is faster than his pull and aim. He takes one. A good one. His left eye and the left rear half of his skull are now gone forever. As is what little spark he had in his miserable life.

Shit. I broke my promise to Jules. We got a dead guy.

I send a quick text to Jules. NO THREAT AT THE CORONATION. ALL CLEAR. SEE YOU SOON. I use all caps so she would be sure to hear me.

I gather up the mortars and put them in the bag that likely brought them up here. I take his phone and wallet, but leave the one-eyed douche for the buzzards. It was a steel air vent cover that blocked the door—I pull it away and head down the stairs with the mortars.

Walking through the lobby, the desk attendant waves. I politely wave back. I will certainly never be back to this hotel. I have burned myself here. The dead douche on the roof has seen to that.

I throw the bag with the mortars in the seat in front and climb in. The road is clear. One big task awaits.

CHAPTER 30

I drove back to the burned out garage. After parking the truck where I first found it and closing the garage door, I began my much-anticipated conversation with the shithead Mistaf.

"So let's set the ground rules. I want to shoot you again; I really, really do. And there are multiple excuses I will use to allow me to do that. Here are a few of them. You listening?" He nodded. "Good. One, if you lie to me. That's going to be an automatic bullet to the other knee. Second excuse, you say "I don't know". That's the same as a lie to me, because I would never insult you by asking you a question you didn't know the answer to. I mean, if nothing else, I have manners. Three, if you say anything bad about the Princess. That one gets you shot twice. You will probably bleed out before I can get you to a hospital. But you'll get to hurt really bad for a long time. So it will be worth it for me. Are we clear?" He nodded emphatically. I ripped the tape from his mouth and it sounded like it hurt.

I turned on the video recorder on my phone, and propped it up against a piece of rubble, capturing Mistaf in all his glory. "First question. What are you doing in this garage?"

"I was instructed to come here to shoot two RPGs at the cathedral."

"Okay. I think you have the hang of this. Now, who instructed you to come here and shoot a rocket at the cathedral?"

"Prince Ta, of Musjistan."

"Man, you're good at this. Why did Ta want you to shoot a rocket at the cathedral?"

"He wanted to kill Princess Jules. He never wants her to take the Throne."

"Feel free to keep adding information to your answers. It will get us out of here faster, eh? Okay, Ta is at the cathedral too. How as he going to avoid getting killed?"

"He was not going to leave the sanctuary for the reception. The rockets were to hit the reception hall only; not the sanctuary. He would be safe in the sanctuary."

"Was there another part to this attack?"

"Yes. One of Ta's security force was to fire two mortars at the reception as well. He was positioned on the roof of the hotel at the bottom of this street. The mortars would ensure mass death and make this look like a terrorist attack. That was the cover Ta was using so the plan would not be detected."

"So Ta expected others to die?"

"Yes. And the more, the better. He believed that the more deaths he caused, the better the guarantee that he would not be caught. The world would assume that the

Muslims attacked in order kill as many Cardinals as possible. To the rest of the world, the Princess would have been seen as an unfortunate unintended victim." As much as I wanted to kill this guy, it didn't come close to my need to kill Ta.

"Last question for now. Who all knows about this plan?"

Ta, Rive from his security force, me, and maybe the King," Whoa.

"The King? Remember what I said about wanting to shoot you. Don't start lying now."

"Ta said the King asked him to kill Jules. I don't know otherwise." This sounded suspiciously like a cover story to make Ta's minions think they were backed by the King.

"So you don't have firsthand knowledge that the King knows? Only what Ta told you?"

"Yes. He said the King wanted Ta to succeed him; not the Princess. He said the King does not trust Jules to protect the fortunes of the Crown."

"Other than what Ta has said, do you have any other information that ties the King to this assassination plot?"

"Only what Ta told me. I have never talked to the King about it or heard him say anything about it. I know that Ta had to spend his own money on the munitions. He did get the King to lease a yacht for the trip, but I do not know if the King did that because of the assassination plot or because Ta is here on an official visit."

"Think very carefully about this next question, because I believe you, but I think you know more than you think you do. Ready?"

"Yes."

"Do you believe that the King is involved in any way with this business? Or do you think Ta made that up to further his personal causes?"

"I truly don't know. If I were to guess, I would say that the King would not harm Princess Jules, under any circumstances. Now could I go to the hospital?"

After erasing Mistaf's last request from the recording, I felt like we could hang Ta. What I didn't know was where the King stood in all this. I needed to talk to Jules.

CHAPTER 31

I arrived at the cathedral with Mistaf laid out on the back floorboard of the club cab. I parked the truck out of sight so as not to alert Ta just yet. I had texted Jules and she was waiting in front with one of her security guys. The other two were close by. One was outside the meeting hall, positioned so he could cover two sides of the building. I couldn't see the other one, but odds were he was at the back of the cathedral, covering the other two sides of the building. The guy with her didn't know it yet, but his next assignment was to take Mistaf to the hospital. Jules had already called Muji, and half a dozen more of her security force were airborne and en route. I had told her enough via text to get her to take care of that part as soon as she could. The extra force would detain Ta and his entourage on her orders, and get them back to Muji. I coaxed her away from the doors and around the side of the cathedral. Couldn't chance Ta seeing us.

Jules had really fixed up for this gig. She looked great. I pulled her aside from her security man.

I whispered "So look. As I'm sure you have deduced, the attack was for today. Mistaf was in a garage ready to shoot two RPGs at the meeting hall. One of Ta's security force was on a hotel roof about a half mile away with two mortars. They were targeted towards the meeting hall as well. We got 'em both, and all the munitions. The threat of attack is over." She hugged me with relief.

"I knew you could do it" she whispered in my ear.

"No. We did it." We broke off the hug, much to my dismay.

"Not me. I've been watching a boring coronation." She let out a nervous little chuckle.

"It was a joint effort. Look, we have some unfinished business. Mistaf is in a truck parked nearby. He needs to get to a hospital. We also have to figure out how we are going to take Ta down. So how about I stay here with you and we figure that out, and one of your security guys takes Mistaf to the hospital?"

"What happened to him?"

"He hurt himself when he was talking to me. So is that a plan?"

"Sure. I guess." She motioned her man over.

"Sesia, we have a situation. I need your discretion and I need you to do exactly as Mr. Buck here tells you. The Crown depends on it. Understand?"

"Yes, Princess Jules. How can I be of service?"

"Here's the keys to a red Silverado. It is parked in an alley between two buildings just over your left shoulder, about 50 feet from here. In that truck is Mistaf, Ta's aide. He tried to kill your Princess today, and I stopped him. He is injured and in need of medical attention. Do you know where the nearest hospital is?"

"Yes. Carpe' Regis Mercy. Here on the island. We are required to know all that type of information as part of our preparation."

"Very well. Take him there and get him treated. Do not let him out of your sight or out of your custody under any circumstances. The Princess here will notify the authorities so that you will not be interfered with. The doctors will insist, but he cannot be admitted to the hospital. Don't worry—he won't die. Just a little gunshot wound."

"I am not worried that he will die. I am worried that he will live. My blade may not be able to resist."

"You'll have to take that up with the Princess. Anyway, when they get him patched up, take him to the condo. Do not question him. And believe nothing he says. Keep him bound and gagged. If anybody shows up at the condo that the Princess has not personally cleared with you, including Ta or any of his security force, shoot them. Is that clear?"

"Yes."

"Can you do all that, to include shooting Ta or any of his men?"

"To protect the Princess and the Crown, yes. I will do anything. I am bound to the Crown and sworn to protect her."

"Good. Then go." He walked briskly towards the truck. I heard the door slam, and the truck pulled out onto the road and sped away.

Time to take care of Ta.

"Jules, we have to take Ta down. How do you want to do that?"

"You have any ideas?"

"We could wait until the reception starts, get his security guys distracted, and I could take him in the sanctuary. He planned on staying there until the bombing was over."

"How do we distract the security force?"

"Well, you're the Crown Princess. Make an excuse to get them into the reception. Ta won't follow. He doesn't want blasted with a mortar. If they refuse your orders, I'll have to make them casualties of Ta's capture. We can't let Ta get away."

CHAPTER 32

Ta saw Jules slip out of the ceremony. What was she doing? Just another embarrassment to the Crown. Hopefully for the last time. He needed her to come back in before the reception. He had to get her in the meeting hall so that he could text Rive and Mistaf and get the fireworks started. He leaned over to the security man sitting with him.

"Wan" he whispered. "Go see what the Princess is doing. Make sure she doesn't leave. Come back and tell me what you see. Hurry."

Wan slipped out of the aisle and moved toward the back of the sanctuary. He could see nothing out of the windows in the front doors. He stepped out to have a look. The Princess was not there. Just then, he saw one of her security force, Sesia, hurrying down the street and into an alley. Then, a red pickup came out of the alley and sped down the street, with Sesia driving. How peculiar that he would leave the Princess? Wan walked towards the side of the cathedral from where Sesia emerged, and peeked around the corner through a large bush. Princess Jules was talking to a strange man, one who Wan had not seen before. His immediate reaction was to protect her, but he sensed that she was at ease. There was no indication of trouble, except for the concerned expression on her face. Wan backed off quietly. He debated a second about whether to make his presence known, out of concern for the Princess, or just report back to Ta. Then he noticed another of the Princess' security force watching her from the back corned of the cathedral. She was protected. He returned to the sanctuary to report back to Ta.

Upon hearing the news from Wan, Ta's senses alerted. Things just didn't seem right. Why would the Princess send her security away, and who was she talking to? He scurried to the back of the sanctuary and into the meeting hall. He called Mistaf. No answer. He dialed Rive. Again no answer. Something wasn't right. He ordered them both to keep their phones close and answer his calls immediately. Time to bolt. Fortunately he had a plan for this eventuality.

CHAPTER 33

Jules went back into the sanctuary and took her seat. She tried to act relaxed, but doubted she was fooling anyone. She let herself glance towards Ta, expecting a condescending look from him for leaving the ceremony. But he wasn't there. She wondered if maybe he took a restroom break? She'd give it a minute. Then she thought again and got up.

She was dialing Buck before she even got out the door. "Buck. Ta isn't in his seat. He may be in the restroom, but I'm not feeling good about this."

"Okay, I know where the men's room is. I'll go in through the meeting hall and check it out."

I came around the building and hurried into the meeting hall and to the restroom door. I could hear nothing. I went in quietly. The place was empty. I ran out of the meeting hall and hooked up with Jules.

"He's not there. He's bugged out. Something must have spooked him. Are his security guys still in the sanctuary."

"Yes"

"Good. That could mean that they aren't in this with him. Could you have one of your guys round them up and have everyone meet back at the condo?"

"Yep. Calling them now."

She spit her orders into the phone. Her guys came around to meet us.

"Any sign of Ta?" I asked.

They replied "No" in unison.

"Did you get hold of Ta's men?"

"We did. They should be on the way any minute."

"Thanks. Let's get the car and go."

On the way, Jules briefed her guys. If they were shocked, they didn't show it. Their instincts had kicked in. I looked at Jules.

"You realize that we have to find him. This problem is not solved until we hand his ass to the King on a platter."

"I know. And I will never feel completely comfortable knowing he is out there somewhere. Now that he has nothing to lose, who knows what he's capable of?"

"I think he's shown you what he is capable of. He was ready to kill dozens of people to cover up your assassination. He's capable alright. I just hope he doesn't have resources here."

"Mistaf may know something."

"Right. That's my hope. Ta may have a provisional worst case scenario plan. If Mistaf knows what that is, we can play the spoiler—again."

"Would he go to the yacht?"

"If it were me, I wouldn't. One, we know about it, and two, it couldn't outrun us. Mistaf has been cooperative. We'll see what he has to say."

"Cooperative huh? Is that why he's at the hospital?"

"Just needed some encouragement. But he came through."

To the security guys "What about Ta's security force. Do you all trust them?"

Neither could guarantee where their loyalty stood. But they were giving them the benefit of the doubt. They knew them well. It was a pretty tight group. I decided that we should be cautious with them, but we definitely needed their help. Jules agreed. This was not the type of thing we could bring the locals in on. It would be a scandal of enormous magnitude for the King.

CHAPTER 34

The condo was alive with activity. At my suggestion, Jules had christened Sesia as kind of the command center boss. He was to stay around the condo and use the Jules' aides to help keep track of everything, while watching Mistaf. He was also charged with keeping the condo secure while the hunt was on. I doubted Ta would show up there, but at this point, nothing could be taken off the table. I gave the aides a crash course on command center recording, and they seemed like they were going to do okay keeping the information catalogued and flowing. We needed to have a central place to coordinate so that we didn't end up chasing each other's tails. Jules pulled me aside.

"Hey."

"Yes Princess?"

"Knock it off. Listen, I know this is my Kingdom's problem, but you have a mission here too."

"And?"

"Everyone is looking to me run this operation, or whatever it is, and I'm not the one to do that. You are."

"So I'll give you any advice that you ask for along the way."

"We don't have the time for me to be running to you every few minutes. Just take over. Please."

"Since you said please…fine. Can you kind of make the announcement? It should come from you."

"Everyone!" she yelled. Complete silence. You could have heard a mouse piss on cotton. "Buck will be taking charge. He is experienced with this type of thing and can get us the best result." She turned to me. "Anything to start with?"

"Sure, thank you Princess. First, we need to make sure that every one of the security force flying in rents their own vehicles. We may need to initiate somewhat of a dragnet, and if so, we'll need all the vehicles we can get. Jules, can one of your aides get the cars reserved? Might save some time."

"Sure thing."

"For the security force here, we're going to match up for now. I'll assign the teams right after this meeting. As soon as we get done talking with all of Ta's force, we're going to canvass some places that they think he may hole up."

"Jules will take over for Sesia and coordinate the aides and the information coming in. We have two aides that know what to do already. They will also be monitoring Mistaf's and Rive's phones. If Ta calls, let them ring. I have some friends that may be able to help us triangulate his location via cell tower pings. Jules, we'll need to evaluate every piece of information we get to see if anything jumps out at us, or if anything correlates with other info. Folks, today there are no coincidences. Everything is important."

"If your assignment takes you away from here, report in frequently to the condo by phone. A text is okay if it can get the message across clearly. Save the phone calls for urgent information. Keep your own notes as well. If this goes on for a while, we'll need to make sure that we're only being redundant when we intend to be."

"Those of you with firearms, meet with Sesia as soon as this meeting is over. We need to know exactly the firepower we have and how much ammunition is on hand. And don't hold back any of your throw guns or reserve ammunition. We don't need any Rambo's on an operation like this." Everybody knows about Sly. Even in Muji.

"We have a simple mission. The objective is to find Ta and detain him. The initial methods we're going to use to make that happen are to create a search grid based our best information as to where he might be; collect and collate information in a manner that gives us the best picture of our current status at any given time; and ensure the people working with us stay safe. Any questions for now?" Silence again. "Okay, let's get to it. Sesia, if you'll collect the firepower data, I'll talk to Ta's security force." To Ta's dudes "Gentlemen? Shall we retreat to the veranda?"

As I feared, Ta's guys had truly little to offer. But I got a feel for them, and one in particular gave me confidence. Call it a feeling, but I read him as straight. I sent him to watch the dock. Ta may try to go to the yacht for something—everything he brought with him is on that boat. Unless he has an emergency cache for a situation like this. I hope not.

If nothing else came from the meeting with his guys, it was that Ta was cagey and ruthless. Why couldn't he be just one or the other?

I sent an email to the Turks with Ta's number. They could track his phone. The problem was I had no real-time communication method with them. It was all done by secure email or the website. I asked in the email if we could change that. A hunt like this needs to have the information as it is created.

CHAPTER 35

Ta went downstairs from the meeting hall and out the rear door. He saw one of Jules men at the corner of the building, so he crouched behind a low wall that ran along the walking path. It allowed him to move down the path unseen. They were looking for threats coming in; it made going out a little easier. The path took him all the way into a residential neighborhood, where he couldn't be seen from the cathedral.

He hurried through the neighborhood, trying to get his bearings. He knew he couldn't go back to the yacht. If they had exposed any part of his plans, they would soon know that he was behind it. He needed to get to the far south end of the island. Two weeks ago he booked a room at a hotel there and prepaid it for a month. He didn't have the money he would have as King, but he had enough for that. His blood boiled at the thought. He would never be King now. Thanks to that little bitch Jules.

He kept dialing Mistaf and Rive, and the phones rang and rang and rang. He had to face the fact that they were no longer with him. All of his escape and evasion plans included Mistaf. The fool. He must have got himself caught. But he will improvise—he can't get caught.

After walking side streets and cutting through residential property for an hour, he stopped in a fuel depot and bought a local map. He was miles away from the hotel. He thought about finding a taxi, but didn't know how well they tracked their fares here. Maybe they had cameras in them, like the ones in Vegas. In the end, his laziness kicked in and he got a cab. It was primitive. Couldn't even pay with a credit card, which he wouldn't do now anyway, but from that he deduced that there were no cameras and no tracking mechanisms.

He paid the cabbie and stepped into the lobby of the hotel. Stupidly, he had used his own name to make the reservation. But it would have to do for now. He got the key and trekked around the building to his room. Outside entrance, like many of the hotels here. He collapsed on the bed and started planning his way off the island. He had checked out a few possibilities around the same time he booked this room. He could ferry over to the mainland, which offered some options. Hop on a puddle jumper to a bordering country. Rent a car and drive as far as he could. Hell, he could hitchhike to the border if he had to. He could get on a merchant ship from the port on this island, or any of the surrounding islands. The ships that came into the small island ports were mostly from the mainland, but they would get him to the big ports on the mainland without going through all the security checkpoints, and there he could find a big vessel. Sail to any place in the world. But whatever route he went, he was convinced that an effective disappearance included getting out of Greece. He decided to sleep on it.

Ta awoke in a panic. His dreams were unsettling because they hit too close to home. In them he was a fisherman. Or a merchant marine. Or a homeless guy begging on a corner. Likely endings, because the one thing that had always plagued him was biting him in the ass again. Money. Oh, he did well enough in Muji because he was part of the Royal Family, so there was always someone willing to pay him for access to the King. And every King permitted the family to work on certain projects, government or otherwise, and he had a steady stream of cash from those looking to win contracts. But the big prize was the Throne. All the riches of the Crown at his disposal. Never to be his. And now, only cash could get him to a safe haven far away. And he might even have enough cash to make that happen. But what would he do when he got there? Get a job? An awful prospect. Maybe become a common thief. Another poor option—he would end up on the run in whatever place he ran away to. There was no good ending for him now that Jules had ruined his life. Oh, he wasn't so egotistical that he didn't accept some of the blame. But the way she jumped ahead of him on the path to the Throne, whether her fault or not, was too much to take. Just wasn't right. His birthright was snatched from him without warning or compassion. He woke up one day, and the Throne was no longer his to have.

Maybe he could kill her anyway? Why not? She was on the island. He was on the island. He could get a gun on the black market and find a way to ambush her. Would they be looking for him to do that? Or would they think he was just trying to get away? He'd have to think about that. But for now he needed to find someplace else to go. It was a big risk staying here under his real name.

There was one computer in the lobby that they generously referred to as a business center. Ta got on it and searched "Rooms to Rent', hoping to come up with something that could shield his identity for the duration of his time on the island. Although he had not admitted his decision, the fact that he was looking for a longer term living situation here was indicative of his base desire: To kill Jules.

He found several ads for rooms on the mainland, but ferry rides back and forth to the island were both risky and costly. He couldn't deplete his cash carelessly. Every dollar he spent had to go towards his purpose. If he rented a room on a longer-term basis, his purpose would be clear. If he just found another hotel for a couple of days, then, in his mind, he was keeping his options open. His web search had also found a hotel down the coast, on the side of the island opposite the yacht, in a much less popular area for tourists. It was cheaper than most. He decided to check it out. He walked out and up the street until he got to a cluster of restaurants and bars, where some taxis hung out for fares, and he hailed one. The driver took him around the country side, through areas that Ta had not yet seen on the island. It was as if they were transitioning from one era to another. The streets became dirt roads. The people went from prosperous and beautiful to weary and ragged. When he got to the hotel, he asked the cabbie to wait and went into the lobby.

If the lobby was indicative of the hotel, it was a dive. The two tattered side chairs didn't match. It was as if they were purchased from a second hand furniture store. The odor in the room was just as unpleasant as it was unrecognizable. If the desk clerk had washed his hair in the past week, it didn't show. This was nothing more than a local dump. Probably rented rooms by the hour. Ta detested everything about it but the price. But he knew the instant that he handed over the first week's rent that his decision was made.

CHAPTER 36

I interviewed Ta's security force one by one, and as a group. It was hastily done, but even with that, it was clear that Ta had shared nothing significant with any of them; except the dead one, of course. There were some tavernas that they knew he liked, but that's where it ended. So we checked them. Our guy at the dock had seen nothing that would trigger suspicion, just as we expected. We then cut the main areas of the island into three sections and our three teams checked what they could. We got back to the condo after midnight. Our canvass of the island yielded nothing.

My next task was to do a complete interrogation of Mistaf. I thought a late-night debriefing when he was sleep deprived could help the process along.

We dug very deeply into the concept that the King may be involved. Both Jules and I came out of it feeling it was simply a ploy by Ta to ensure full cooperation from Ta and Rive. But we couldn't be sure. Other than that, Mistaf was a blank. He claimed no knowledge about any provisions Ta may have made in case the plan went awry. Everything else we already knew, thanks to SIC. I had Jules leave us while I asked Mistaf one last question.

"You understand that I have to be absolutely sure that you are telling us everything you know, right?"

"Yes. I've told you everything I know."

I get that you say that. But I have to be sure. For me to be sure, I have to hurt you, and keep hurting you until I know you couldn't have held out. It's the only way." He actually whimpered. "It's going to be bad. Just the way it has to be. But I have to be sure."

"No, no. I've told you everything. I'll help you catch him! I'll do anything! I'll tell the King everything! Please!" His fear was genuine, judging by the urine seeping through his pants. That was all I needed.

"Everything okay?" Jules asked as I came into the kitchen.

"Yep. Sent a couple of the security guys in there to get Mistaf a clean pair of pants. He told us everything he knows."

"What did you do now?"

"Checked his bladder. It's fine." Hands on her hips, her look was very stern. "Seriously, he's fine. I didn't do anything."

As usual, the SIC did not disappoint. I had been up all night, but let the security force alternate with naps so they would be as fresh as possible. I was watching my phone in anticipation of hearing from the Turks. At 5:15 in the morning, the email came. They had been able to track Ta's phone, but unfortunately the island had only two cell towers. With only two towers off of which to ping, his signal could not be triangulated. It could be narrowed somewhat, based on which tower pinged earliest when his phone was being used, but that only narrowed his location down to one side of the island or the other. That sounded like a big help at first, but then we realized that he could be ten yards closer to one tower than the other, and his location would look the same as if he were right next to one of the towers. However, we would know when he made calls and shortly thereafter, and who he made them to. He had made four calls since the noon yesterday; two each to Mistaf and Rive. We already knew that, and knew the times the calls were made, but I was hoping the Turks could tell us where Ta was when he made them, but the tower situation prevented any real tracking. The Turks also ran Ta's name through every known database in Greece to see what they could come up with, and got a hit on a hotel on the south side of the island. He had made a reservation there several weeks ago. That was both good news and bad. Good, because we had a lead on Ta. Bad because it proved that he had made provisions in case of a problem.

I roused the guys. Left two of the security force at the condo and mobilized the rest with me. The hotel was but a few miles away, and we were parked around the corner from it in less than five. The Turks, God Bless 'em, even had the room number. I sent two guys around to protect the rear window—the room was on the second floor, so he could theoretically make the jump to the ground. I took one with me and we went to the door. In other times, I would have gone to the desk and strong-armed a key, but since I didn't know how long we would be on the island, I felt it best not to land on the most wanted list of the local police just yet. Ear to the door, I listened for a minute. Separating the sounds, I blocked the whisper of the light breeze; the hum of the air conditioning and the mini-fridge in the room; and the breathing of my partner. Unless he was dead, Ta wasn't in there. I picked the locked and went in to have a look.

There was nothing here. No clothes, no toiletries, nothing. He had either moved already, or had nothing but the clothes on his back. If he planned well enough to have a hotel room paid for in advance, then he likely would have also planned for provisions such as clothing, weapons, cash, transportation, etc. Otherwise, what good would the hotel room do him? I went to the window and gave an all clear signal to the security guys and then down to the lobby.

The desk clerk was willing, but had limited information. It cost me fifty American just to find out that Ta had not checked out, but had not been seen since late yesterday afternoon. I saw a computer in the lobby and checked out the browser history. It had been deleted. That made me suspicious, so I got the internet signature, or whatever the hell it's called, from the desk clerk, and I sent it to the Turks.

We were at a dead end. Nothing else to check for now. If I knew what else Ta's back-up plan entailed, I might have a clue as to where to look next. I decided that the yacht was the best chance, so I left a man to watch the hotel, and the rest of us headed to the dock.

CHAPTER 37

The skiff was still tied to the dock, so we loaded up and took it to the yacht. I left a guy on the shore to watch for Ta, or in case Jules called and needed someone immediately. We didn't know what to expect in terms of intel, so it was good to always have a couple of guys at the ready. The six extra security guys had been forced to stay at the airport overnight—they got in late and the car rental agency was closed. They would be on the island within an hour. I needed the reinforcements.

The yacht crew was helpful, but ignorant. They thought the munitions they took on for Ta was a big box of kiwis and figs that were smuggled out of Bulgaria. Mistaf told them that Musjistan Customs would not permit the bulk sale of certain fruits. The crew didn't care one way or the other about fruit. The hold was locked, so they never saw the box again until Mistaf and Rive carried it off the yacht. Otherwise, they gave their passengers the privacy they paid for. We searched the yacht for any clue Ta may have left. It was obvious that everyone had planned to come back to the yacht. Other than that little tidbit, the yacht was a dead end. We packed up everything to take to the previous passengers who were now residents of the condo. The crew wanted to know what they should do. I considered whether we might catch Ta trying to get back to the yacht, and determined that no, it would be a waste of resources to watch it. So I sent the yacht and crew home. I left a man on the shore to watch them until they were out of sight, just as a precaution, and that was the end of the yacht.

Back at the condo, I divided up the crews. The six new force members had arrived and were ready. They had chartered a private jet, so they were able to bring their weapons too. Apart from Jules and me, there were 20 souls on the scene now. Twelve were security force members. The three remaining from Ta's team were no longer under any suspicion—there was simply no indication that he had included them in anything devious. The two porters and four hookers from the yacht were useless. I would have sent them back with the yacht, but not knowing where their loyalties lie, I opted to have a security man take them to the mainland and put them on a plane back to Muji. We alerted the security there to tag them on arrival and isolate them until this mess was cleaned up. Jules' aides had proven their worth, trading off on their command center duties and doing an admirable job. I had spent more time with them overnight, and was confident that they knew enough to know what they didn't know. That meant that they would make sure I got anything that they didn't recognize as routine, and would get it in a hurry.

The condo slept eight comfortably, had four bathrooms and a huge kitchen, so I designated that as the living quarters for those who needed to rest or freshen up, and we moved the Ta operation headquarters to my apartment. Ta had no way of tracking the apartment, or me for that matter, so I made Jules promise to stay there, and only there, unless she was with me. She agreed, but in her normal reluctant fashion. She always resists special treatment. It seems like all the really special ones do.

The security man that I had left to watch Ta's hotel room had seen nothing. We could afford to keep someone there a little longer since we had a bigger team now, so I sent his relief to the hotel and him to the condo to get some rest. About that time, an email popped up from the SIC. Ta's phone had been silent, but the browser history on the hotel computer was telling. It searched for rooms to rent on the island and mainland, and there was a hit on virtually every hotel on the island. While it didn't really narrow down Ta's location, it told me that he was planning to see this through. The only reason he had to stay here was to kill Jules. And that shit was not going to happen on my watch.

CHAPTER 38

Most people would be unnerved when told that a madman had decided to risk everything for the opportunity to kill them. Jules was not shaken by the revelation in the least—acted like I had just asked her about the weather. She'll be a great queen. I told her that she had to take this threat seriously.

"I'm safe. Ta doesn't know about this apartment. He doesn't even know if I'm still on the island. And he doesn't know about my secret weapon." She flashed a coy grin.

"I'm glad you think this is so funny. He's running around loose, and we don't know where. Would you think about going back to Muji?"

"And take this threat home to the King? No thanks. Besides, the only place in the world that Ta might have an ally is in Muji. If there were an advantage to be had for him, it would be there."

"He could go there anyway. Did you think of that."

"Not really. But now that I have, I've got to do something."

"What's that? Have you decided to plug in the King?"

"Oh God no. Not until we get Ta. I don't believe that the King was in on this, but the way to guarantee that is to take Ta back home."

"What will that prove?"

"First, we'll see if Ta sticks to his story in front of the King. If he does, it's incumbent upon the King to have this whole situation investigated independently—pull out all the stops to expose any possibility of a conspiracy beyond Ta. It will be pretty suspicious if he doesn't. But if not, I'll get my own people on it. If there is something that comes back to the King, I'll find it. I may not be able to do anything about it, but I'll know. And if the threat remains credible, I'll go on a long holiday until the King is dead. I may even have a spot for a new head of security, if you're interested."

I let that last comment pass. "You've thought this through."

"Of course. You think I'm just another pretty face?" It certainly was a pretty face. "As I was saying, I need to do something. I need to let Ta know that I am still on the island. I don't want him going to Musjistan. Who knows what he would try to do there."

"Not a good idea. Under the radar, now that's a good idea for you."

"I'll still be well hidden. But if he knows I'm still here, he'll stay here. And that's what we need him to do."

"I think we have had this conversation before; you know, about making yourself the bait."

"We have. I was right then, and I'm right now." I hate arguing with her.

CHAPTER 39

Holing up in a rent-by-the-hour fleabag hotel was not how Ta envisioned any part of his life. He was on the lamb, as they say: eating gas station roller food and convenient store pre-packaged garbage because restaurants posed an exposure risk. Same with taxis—when feasible, he walked instead of taking a cab. But the one advantage this seedy existence offered was that his low-rent hotel was located in a low-rent part of the island, populated with some of the low-rent shady types that come with the territory. He had made a contact on the streets that said they could get him a pistol.

He was searching for a contact, so Ta frequented some places that he anticipated could produce one. One night he was in a local dive bar, staying in the shadows as much as he could, when a candidate caught his eye. Two illicit looking guys were at a table in the back of the bar talking very low with one another. They kept looking around every couple of minutes, clearly not wanting anyone to hear their conversation. Low life for sure. Money was exchanged, and one of them left the bar. The other was finishing his beer, so Ta seized the opportunity and walked to his table.

"Good evening." The miscreant looked at Ta like he had two heads.

"You want something buddy? I'm kind of busy here." He obviously wasn't busy—just didn't like the attention from an unknown.

"Maybe. I'm looking for something and I need a little guidance."

"And what would that be?"

"Well, first, you need to know that it may not be exactly legal."

"Do you have money? That can trump the law sometimes."

"I might."

"Well then, why don't you give me a little hypothetical of what you might be looking for, and maybe I can help."

"Okay. If a guy were looking for a pistol where might he get one?"

"That's perfectly legal. He would go to the government offices, apply for a permit, get on the waiting list, pick out a suitable gun, suffer the waiting period, and then go pick it up and register it. It would be all yours in about two months, providing you were a citizen and your reasons for applying had something to do with national security."

"Let's say the guy didn't have two months and national security was not at issue. What then?"

"He might talk to an entrepreneur such as I."

"And what would that entrepreneur do for him?"

"He would probably ask him if he had 100 Euros."

"And if the guy did?"

"Then the entrepreneur would make arrangements to meet him at midnight two days from now across the street in the gas station parking lot. That is, if he coughed up 50 Euros now and promised another 50 upon delivery."

"That could be arranged. You want the money here or outside?"

Two days later, Ta waited in the parking lot of that gas station. It was about a mile from his hotel. It was just after midnight, and the place had closed several hours ago. His contact was on island time, so predictably late. Ta was wearing a floppy fisherman's hat and a light jacket to help him blend better, compliments of a $12 purchase at a second hand store. Most of the people he came into contact with knew he was out of place, but they didn't seem to care as long as they weren't bothered.

The thrift store visit also garnered a wide belt that he could use to secure the pistol to his body. The belt he wore to the coronation was one of those thin little dress belts—useless for holding a pistol in place at your waist.

The broker entered the parking lot from the back of the gas station. Ta went to meet him, wanting to be as far from the roadway as possible. "The money."

"Here. It's all there."

"Then you won't mind if I count it." He took a minute to leaf through the bills. "Okay. Here you go."

Ta took the plastic grocery bag and looked in. A revolver, probably older than Ta. "Is it loaded?"

"No good if it's not, is it?"

Ta fumbled with the cylinder until he found the latch and flipped it open.

"You sure you know how to handle that thing?"

"Of course." The cylinder was full. "Any more bullets?"

"You didn't ask for ammo. I suppose you should feel lucky that it came with any."

Ta closed the cylinder, pointed the gun in the guy's face, and pulled the trigger. The bang was louder than he expected. This guy had sold his last gun. He lay faceless in the parking lot. Ta took the money off his dealer, ran behind the gas station and made his way to the hotel.

Ta got back to the room and hid the gun on the molded ledge under the bathroom sink. Not highly creative, but he'd never hidden a gun before. He had hated to use the bullet, but he needed to know that the gun worked. Destroying a potential witness was just a perk. The dude's life was shit anyway. In Ta's twisted mind, he probably did the guy a favor.

Now he had a gun. One step closer.

As time passed, Ta wasted most of his days sitting in the room. He couldn't risk going outside to any extent; every journey into the public eye increased the potential for him to be burned. He had no doubt that someone was after him—he just didn't know who. The Greek police? Members of the King's force? Interpol? The media was completely dark; not a single story about anything related to him or Jules or Muji. Mistaf and/or Rive had talked, he was certain of it. Whatever agency they had informed to had chosen to keep this quiet. But they were out there. He knew it.

For every minute in that wretched room, he loathed Jules that much more. Ultimately, he had to figure out a way to get to her. Her condo was out of the question. One, she may no longer be staying there and two, if she was, the security would be tight. He had to formulate a plan to bring Jules out into the open. He'd keep checking the media and the internet. An opportunity would present itself soon enough. It had to.

CHAPTER 40

Another idea that I hated, courtesy of Princess Jules. She contended that we should forge ahead with the remainder of her official appearances. The Coronation went off without a hitch; no one was the wiser about the assassination attempt. And if Jules was missed at the reception, it didn't cause a stir; she hadn't heard anything from the King. So her assertion was that she should act as if nothing had happened and draw Ta out of hiding. We debated the merits of her conclusion, and I finally convinced her to forego the Council meeting. But she was firm on her commitment to attend the opera debut and be seen in public. She sent all the press outlets, both on the island and on the mainland, a release announcing that the King of Musjistan was sending the Crown Princess to celebrate the opening of the Russian Opera in Greece. It wasn't the lead story anywhere, but it made the newspapers and the internet. I was in favor of having her presence reported *after* she had attended the opera, so Ta wouldn't know for sure where she was going to be at any certain time. But she contended that Ta needed confirmation that she was still on the island. She feared that if Ta waited around too long with no prospects of finding her, he might just think it wasn't worth the risk and get the hell out of Dodge—be gone forever. I think subconsciously she may have wanted to push the issue to bring it to a conclusion. Maybe not the best tactical move, but I saw the merits. Had it been a target that I wasn't sleeping with, I may have thought more favorably of the scheme.

I took three of the security force to help with the recon of the opera house. They had proven themselves both capable for the work and loyal to the Princess. We needed to know the where and how of a prospective attempt on Jules. Lives, especially one in particular, could depend our preparation.

My instinct was that Ta had either stowed some type of firearm with his emergency provisions, or had a contact to obtain one if needed. It would be small arms, as he blew his financial wad on the RPGs and mortars; that much we knew for sure. Neither the SIC nor any of the security force had any knowledge that Ta had ever trained with any firearms. That drastically narrowed his choice of weapons. The safe bet was a pistol of some type. The odds of Ta becoming proficient enough to make a kill shot to a moving vehicle or from some distant perch played heavily against the possibility of a sniper rifle. So my decision was to recon hardest for a pistol shot, but check out the obvious sniping contingencies.

I laid out the route and timed the trip. The most predictable part was the ferry. We could possibly take a ferry to another island, and then ferry from there to the mainland, but that posed separate risks. One, if Ta was watching the docks that day, he would see what ferry the Princess got on, giving him total assurance that she would be on the ferry coming from the pother island. He could guarantee her arrival time and point. It also exposed the Princess for a much longer period of time. So we settled on the ferry straight to the mainland. We had not yet settled on the exact time—it ran eight times per day.

Ferry trip and all, we were 70 minutes door to door. Not sure we'd use the exact route we took on the mainland, but others would be similar. Since public thoroughfares provide so many locations for ambush opportunities, the best choice is to make your route unknown—to the point of scuttling plans at the last minute and changing the route. In this case, there were several options once we got off the ferry. I would continue to study them overnight.

The opera house stands alone in a sort of commercial district. It is circular, as are so many structures in Greece, and large, about the size of a typical hockey arena in the U.S. It was recently erected for a building here in the Old Country, and the architects thought enough about parking to locate it where parking space was adequate to accommodate the vehicles of a few thousand patrons. This was not the norm in the metropolitan areas of Greece—cars weren't a big thing when Greek commerce was on the rise.

There were eight entrances to the opera house. Two of them were designated as staff or performer entrances. The six double-wide public entrances emptied into a spacious hallway that ran around the seating area from about where the stage began on one side of the building to the same reference point on the other side. There were four doors from the hallway into the seating area—all bigger than the exterior doors.

There was a standard door for performers and employees in the very back of the building, behind the stage. The office staff had a single-door side entrance. That door led to offices, and there were secured doors between the offices and the hallway. Bottom line—there were lots of ways to get into that theatre.

The access to the balcony was, thankfully, via steps from inside of the seating area. I would have to account for that area as well.

We could ostensibly cover every exterior entrance, which would dedicate all but four of the security force to doors. The remaining four would have to cover the close-quarters responsibilities for Jules, the entire seating area of the theatre, and the interior entrances. Some of the posts might have roving responsibilities also. I would need to determine which areas lent themselves to this without compromising Jules' safety. None of this was ideal, but it would have to do.

We knew where the Princess would be seated, and we had to assume Ta did as well. I reconned all of the vantage points and scoped out the various escape routes. Egress would not be simple. There was the challenge of navigating a packed house. And if attacking from somewhere other than in the crowds, the possible locations were either in the rafters over the stage or on the right side of the orchestra pit. Both the rafters and the pit are away from exits. Ta would have to go across the pit or around the stage if he shot from the pit; or down a series of ladders and stairs if coming out of the rafters. Thankfully, the rafters only offered one area with a clear enough path to Jules' seat for a shot. I would either post a man in the rafters or search the rafters before the show and assign one of the roving guys to keep an eye on the stairs.

Emergency medical services were two miles from the opera house. If Jules or someone on the team needed care, we could count on getting them attended to in five minutes. If Ta needed medical care, well, good luck to him.

We finished up and returned to the ferry via a different route. I liked this one better. The roadside ambush points were fewer and the traffic was sparse. I'd have to look at this one closely tonight. We pulled on to the ferry and I checked out the boat again. If we were strategic about where parked the car that Jules was to ride in, it would be tough for Ta to get to it on the ferry. I estimated where we had to be in line to get the perfect roost—under the pilot house, towards the front of the ferry. We could make that happen without too much trouble.

CHAPTER 41

Back at the apartment, I brief Jules. I wanted her to know everything. I planned on having someone next to her the entire time, but if things went to hell and she was put in a situation where no one was with her, I wanted her to know what her options were. We went over the routes on the island, the routes on the mainland, the ferry, the opera house. We programmed local taxi numbers into her phone. I gave her the extra set of keys for each of the rental vehicles to carry in her clutch. She was a quick study and asked good questions. The bottom line: Get back to the apartment as fast as possible if on the island or the ferry coming to the island; or go to the closest local police if on the mainland or ferry going to the mainland. I gave her the exact locations of the two police barracks that came into play on the mainland, and she rattled them back to me. Her memory is excellent and she didn't need to take notes, which was good; if she got in a situation where she needed to get to safety with none of us around, urgency would preclude the luxury of referring to notes.

The SIC had nothing new. No leads on where Ta might be. His phone had gone completely silent. It caused me to wonder: If he had no phone charger, that would indicate a lack of preparation and therefore a lack of resources. But what if he had packed a back-up phone? Or bought a burner? I couldn't get a handle on how well he was prepared, or wasn't prepared. That made my job much harder. I had to plan for both conditions every step of the way. My skills were being tested. Under other circumstances, I would relish the challenge. But in this case, the threat to Jules took all the fun out of it.

The security detail had cleared a local market and as a result, Jules' aides were able to shop earlier in the day. They put together a nice meal that evening. We ate at the apartment in two shifts—it wasn't big enough to handle the whole group at once. I met with the full security force after supper and went over the assignments and responsibilities for tomorrow. I considered them all interchangeable. Each needed to know what was expected from everyone.

The only comfort in this night was the two hours I spent with Jules. She had a way of making the rest of the world disappear. Another of her multiple talents.

"How do you feel about tomorrow?". Her head was resting on my chest and I could almost feel the gears turning.

"We'll keep you safe. These guys would die for you, and we've done the work. We're ready. How do you feel about tomorrow?"

"I'm not worried. Never have been. I am an idealist—good prevails over evil, right? And we are good—you are good."

"Thanks."

"You know we need Ta alive?"

"You keep reminding me." I've never wanted to kill anyone as bad as I want to kill Ta. "You keep telling me how much you want him to live."

"I don't necessarily want him to live. I just want to know if the King is involved in this. The only way we will ever know for sure is to take Ta back to Muji."

"You know, I kind of like the "long holiday" idea you proposed earlier. We could spend that time together while you waited for your grandfather to die." That was a little crass.

"I don't want to be away from my grandfather unless I know he was involved. I pray that he's innocent in all this. And you should too."

"You mistake my desire for being isolated with you as wanting your grandfather to be corrupt."

"Can you be serious? If the King is involved, don't you know what that means to my Country? Another corruption among the Royals. A scandal that could cause Parliament to denounce the Royal family and delay ascension to the next generation, or longer. We could go decades without a ruler, allowing the politicians to feast on the opportunities. They are every bit as greedy as those you have in America."

"Then we should kill them all. That's the only cure. I can tell you that from experience." She shot a look of disgust at me.

"Stop. Please. I need to talk this out with you. You're all I have—my only confidant. But you keep deflecting with your sarcasm."

"I do, and I apologize. My way of coping."

"Well don't cope right now. Just talk to me."

"Fair enough. We save you, catch Ta, and take him before the King. We're on the same page." I still wasn't as convinced that taking Ta back to Muji would clear everything up. But she knew her King better than I.

"And you are full of it. I know how you really feel. But I also know you'll do what's best. So you understand that the Parliament has powers that can be enacted when they can prove that the Royals have gone off the rails?"

"Tell me about that."

"Exposing a plan to assassinate the direct heir, and implicating the King in the plot, would be all they needed to remove the King and implement Parliamentary rule. Parliamentary rule would last until they voted it out, or the vote expired. The vote can expire only after all the original voters are out of Parliament. It's a legitimate threat to the Royal Lineage."

"Then it's something that we cannot let happen."

"Correct. If, God forbid, the King is in on this, then he must be convinced to step down: He must abdicate voluntarily for the sake of the Crown. Maybe I can get him to do that. Parliament must never know about his corruption."

Okay. I understand what we're working towards and what is at risk."

"Thank you. It's important to me that you do. Now could you just kiss me so I can go to sleep?" A request I'll never argue with.

CHAPTER 42

Ta read the news with objectivity. He could ill afford to be fooled. Too much on the line. Is she really stupid enough to expose herself? Or was it a trap? And if it is a trap, is there a way to beat it?

The opera had been on Jules' schedule since just before Ta made the trip to Greece. She was supposed to attend on behalf of the King. He thought she would cut and run after the smoke cleared from the assassination attempt. But she stayed. He thought about it to himself.

'She's trying to impress the King. She's told him that I tried to have her killed, but she will complete her Royal tasks nonetheless. What a suck-ass. So easy for her. She has a security force, and I have only me. She has all the resources of the Crown; I'm living in a shit hole and eating out of gas stations. She will go back to Muji and live a life of luxury—the life I was to live. And I'm forced to run away and live on nothing. But I have a gun, and I have the brains. And when I find an opening, she'll have a reckoning. If not the opera, then somewhere else.'

Ta began to formulate a plan. A fairly good one, he thought. It had kinks, but they could be worked out with some thought and preparation, and a good disguise. He had to get busy though—the Russian opera opened in two days.

His plan started with a visit to the opera house. He had seen some posters around the island advertising a local production—tonight was the last night. He needed to go. He hopped a ferry to the mainland and navigated the streets on foot for the better part of an hour. He made it to the center of town and found a taxi to take him the rest of the way. By the time they pulled up at the opera, the show was started. Just as Ta expected. He didn't have a ticket and didn't plan on buying one. He walked up to the main door and asked the attendant what was playing, even though he knew.

"The Barber of Seville" the usher said. "Tonight's the last show."

"I would have loved to see that, but it's not in the budget this month."

"It's been a hit. All local talent, too."

"Nice. Wish I could catch a glimpse." The usher was silent. "Would you mind if I peeked in? Just for a second?" The usher was viably weighing the pros and cons of the request in his head.

"I suppose it couldn't hurt—but for only a couple of seconds, okay?"

"Yes, of course. I really appreciate this."

The usher led him through the hallway to the closest set of doors and cracked one side so that Ta could see in. It was a nice setting—plenty of comfortable seating, large stage, state-of-the-art lighting. Balcony and floor seating, loges across the front and raised private balconies on both ends of the loge aisle. He would have liked to see more, but he couldn't raise the suspicions of the usher. He backed out of the door. "Thanks very much," his gratitude only partially feigned.

"Glad to help. Maybe next time you can see an entire production."

"I sure hope to. Thanks again." And Ta was out. He had seen what he needed to.

He visited the second-hand store again. Racks and racks of any sort of clothing that someone could get a price for. And cheaply sold. He strolled around the store, trying to look casual. If his idea was going to work, this part was crucial. And then he saw something that brought his entire plan together.

CHAPTER 43

It was time. Mistaf was secured and gagged; his guards would be Jules' aides. We left one Beretta 9mm with them that, after a quick crash course, both could shoot well enough to hit center mass from close range. Not ideal, but nothing I could do about it. Jules' safety was paramount, so the security force had to be with her. Besides, the chances of Mistaf breaking free and overpowering the aides with his bad knee were slim. There was a chance that Ta may show up, but again, only a slight one. We had been extremely careful to hide our comings and goings, so there was no reason to suspect that Ta even knew about the apartment.

Jules was looking spectacular in her formal gown. No one would be watching the Russians jumping around in their tights—they'd all be staring at Jules.

The security force was ready. We had gone over all the contingencies any of us could think of. But the possibilities were endless, because we had no idea of Ta's resources. The only thing we were reasonably sure of was that Ta didn't have a bunch of money to spend to hire an assassin. The Turks had heard no chatter about anyone being hired for a job either. It wasn't a lock, but the odds were very good that Ta would have to do this thing himself. And we were hoping that he saw the opera as his last good opportunity.

This was an exposure risk for me. I generally didn't parade around in convoys with security teams and princesses. But I had been careful not to use any of my typical resources—communication had been limited to the SIC. I had not procured special weapons or requested technical assistance as on some other jobs. The Turks had proven their trustworthiness. So there should be no blip on anyone's screen about where I was or what I was doing. At least I hoped not.

We took three vehicles. I would have preferred armor plating, but there was none available on such short notice. The first car was all security force. I rode in the second with Jules and two other security guys. The trail vehicle was all security force, like the lead one. We got to the ferry early and allowed the right amount of cars to board in front of us so that we could park in the ideal area for the cruise.

The vistas on the water were inspiring. Jules never missed the chance to comment on them. "What a waste of these awesome views—me holed up in my car. I feel like I'm letting Ta control me."

"To an extent, you are. Has to be that way for now. But it won't be like this much longer", I lied. Who really knew?

"And what if he doesn't show himself? I just go home and leave him to do whatever?"

"What can he do? Sneak into Muji? He's too well known there to try that. He'd be spotted in a minute."

"Not if he got a fake identity and disguised himself."

"He would never get close to you. Your security force are real pros." I knew only too well that anyone could be had. I just didn't want her worrying about that right now. "Besides, if we don't catch him while you're still in Greece, I'll take some time off and find him."

"And how do you propose to do that?"

"Let's just say it's what I do."

"I know so little about you."

"But you know *me*. That's the important thing." This crisis had allowed me to glaze over the details of my life. That wouldn't hold up after this was all over. But mercifully, the ferry was docking, and our conversation was put on hold. I loved being with Jules, but I could never fully confide in her. That was just how my life had to be. I had come to grips with that reality long ago.

Something sparked in my mind during our conversation. I couldn't quite put my finger on it yet, but it was there. I'd have to figure that out.

CHAPTER 44

I had decided on a back way to the opera house using secondary streets. It was a low-traffic route we had used during recon; they were decent roads and it wouldn't take much longer than the main road. There were a couple of places that lent themselves to an ambush, but it would take vehicles and heavy arms to stop our convoy. So all in all a fairly good choice.

The trip from the dock to the opera house came off without a hitch. After stopping in front of the main entrance, we surrounded the door to shield the Princess as she stepped out of the car. I didn't prefer the main entrance, but it was the only one we could get close to with a vehicle. The risk of using this entrance was offset by the low amount of exposure Jules would have from the car to the door. Much like a football huddle around the quarterback, we enveloped the Princess and chauffeured her to the door. We handed our tickets to the usher and stopped in the hall to evaluate the surroundings before we started towards the seats. I would be sitting with Jules. Security men would be at every entrance, and the man assigned to the rear door would watch the stage area as well. One man would be positioned at the base of the stairs to the rafters; two others on the main floor, one of which would have a view of the balcony stairs. As I scanned the hallway, four of the security force moved out. Two of them would check the rafters and the other two, the orchestra pit, before they all assumed their assigned post. I didn't have the luxury of alerting the police for obvious political reasons. And the opera had no security of any kind. There had never been a reason for it. So it was all on us.

We got texts from the two forward teams saying that all was clear. The rafters and pit were clean, and the men were in position. We started for our seats. We moved down the aisle, Jules with all the grace of the Queen she would someday be. The lights were still up, so she was noticed immediately, and you could see the hum spreading around the audience like the wave at a football game.

We got to our seats. As the guest of Greek's First Lady, Jules was given a loge near the front right of the stage. There were other loges around us, and those seated in them all seemed kosher—none were Ta. As the lights went down, my senses went up. But something still sat in the recess of my mind that I couldn't retrieve.

My mind kept working as I kept watch. Now that I was actually sitting in the audience, what are the weaknesses? How would someone be able to get close enough to Jules in here to shoot Jules and still get away? The place was packed. If Ta was sitting in this audience somewhere, he would have to expose himself before he could get close enough to be a serious threat with a pistol. A rifle had been all but ruled out when we cleared the rafters and the orchestra pit—just too bulky to be carrying around a theatre unnoticed. The topic had been exhausted during our meetings and we concluded that, if the rafters and pit were clean, a pistol was only remaining option for a shooter in this setting. I was comfortable that our conclusions were good to that point. What we hadn't figured out, and what the challenge would be for Ta, was how he would get close enough to Jules for a kill shot and then escape after the shot. He would have to plan his getaway; no possibility that an ego like Ta's would let him chance this being a suicide mission. His ego also gave us another advantage—he would be overconfident in his plan, and that meant he wouldn't see its weaknesses until it was too late. I hoped.

CHAPTER 45

Ta had outsmarted them. Of all the things they would be prepared for, this one could not have been on their radar. It wasn't on his radar until he saw the old theatre usher coat on the rack at the thrift store. It was ragged, but with the lights down in the opera, no one would notice. It was the same deep maroon color, similar buttons, about the same length. The cut was far from exact, but it looked much like the one the usher was wearing that so kindly permitted him a peek into the opera house. He was sure he could score the matching hat once he got in the building.

It all came together when he rushed up to the back door. "Sorry I'm late. Had a flat tire" he explained to the usher tending the door. "No problem, but you better hurry. The show has started." As Ta hurried past, his coat registered with the usher as being wrong. But before he could turn and make his challenge, his lights went out.

Ta used the revolver to swipe a hard blow to the back of the usher's head. He collapsed, and something skittered across the floor—a pencil flashlight.

Every usher in the world owned one. Ta snatched it up, drug the usher away from the door, and stuffed him behind some props. It was dark enough that no one would find him until after the opera. Ta then grabbed the usher's round red hat—looked like a bellhop's. He considered taking the coat as well, but the guy was much smaller than Ta. The old coat might get noticed, but he had to be able to move freely, so he passed on the usher's coat. The dark would have to do the rest. Suddenly, there was a break in the music—a dramatic pause for effect—and Ta heard footsteps. Someone was coming. He moved quickly behind the very props where he stowed the usher, and watched as one his security force walked by, obviously patrolling the area. Traitorous bastard. What Ta would do to him if he ever got the chance. But for now, he needed to stay clear of him. And there were sure to be others, so Ta tread softly as he came out of his hiding spot.

He didn't know anything about the Russian opera, but he knew that the show had started some ten minutes ago. It was too dark for him to really see much, so the flashlight was a good acquisition. He walked around the hall behind the stage until he found a door. He opened it and peeked in, not knowing what to expect. To his surprise, it was a stage entrance for performers. He walked in, and could see through the left side of the stage, out onto the seating area. He was behind opaque curtains, and obscured from the view of the audience. He knew this because a handful of performers were back there with him, awaiting their cues to enter the fray. He parted the curtains slightly, and found that it gave a good view of the audience. He took the opportunity to scan the crowd. The Princess would have premium seating, so he searched out the balconies and loges first. She was not in any of the balcony boxes. The loges spanned across the front of the orchestra pit, the entire width of the theatre. Starting from his right, he studied every box. And there she was, in a loge to his left, down in the front and near the left side of the theatre. None of the security men were in her box. There was one other guy there he didn't recognize. He was seated and Ta couldn't tell much about the guy. Perhaps he was the guy Wan had seen talking to Jules outside of the cathedral the day of the coronation. Was he going to be a problem, or was he just some man-whore Jules picked up on the island? Not really like her, but who knows? Shouldn't really matter. Maybe he'll just shoot him too.

The hall behind the stage led to either side of the theatre. The doors between the public areas and backstage were crash-bar equipped; they opened from the stage side, but were locked on the public side. Ta decided to go through the one to the left of the stage. He peeked through the stage door and waited until he saw the security man heading back the other way.

His newly developed plan required him to get back through the crash-bar door, so he rummaged around the area until he found a piece of wood; fortuitous for him that they built props back there. He propped the door open and made his way around the hallway to a door that entered the theatre just behind the loges. He would enter the seating area to the right of Jules. His disguise would allow him to walk right up behind her and take the shot. The shot would create panic, and all the security force would run to the shot to catch Ta trying to escape through the crowds—but they would be too late. From the aisle, he could be out the door in seconds and then through the stage door, closing it behind him. Anyone chasing would have to wait for a key or someone backstage to open the door. If any security men remained back there, his disguise would get him by—he'd just duck his head and keep moving. He could then exit the building through the door he came in, and would disappear through the back lot and into the adjoining business district, just a few blocks from a row of restaurants. Before the police could even get there, he would have reached the restaurants and hailed a taxi. Then start his journey to a new life.

As he gathered his nerve, he wondered about how good this new existence would be without any money. There had to be someplace that a smart guy like him could go and make money without having to punch a time clock, or do any real work for that matter. He would decide that later. Right now he needed to find the courage to kill a Crown Princess, knowing that the King would not rest until he was tracked down and brought to justice. But it was worth the risk. He was going to be hunted anyway, for the failed assassination attempt. He might as well make the hunt worth their effort.

There was no life for him in Muji, and he would suffer every day for the rest of his life with the knowledge that the Princess bested him. At least he would have the satisfaction of knowing that she would never take the Throne.

CHAPTER 46

I've found the opera to be enjoyable the few times I've attended. The costumes don't do much for me, but the story lines are pure: jilted lovers, revenge, rich against the poor. It seems that you understand the story even if you don't understand the language. That was the case here, and under different circumstances, I would have appreciated the talent, the power of the voices, and the tragedy of the story. But I had my own tragedy to worry about.

Jules had reached for my hand as soon as the theatre darkened, holding it tightly as she pretended to be contently watching the show. But I could tell she was on high alert. As tensions rose, I was more and more into my element. Like the firemen that run into a building that everyone else is running out of, I find myself immersing into impending danger. An inescapable tool of those that succeed in my trade. I am able to see what I need to see. The lights from the stage help some, but by this time my eyes have adjusted to the darkness. I have heard nothing but the opera; nothing to signal problems. So I wait, still trying to extract that evasive tidbit of information hidden somewhere in my brain. For some reason, it feels like the key to this whole situation. I take myself back through the conversation with Jules in an attempt to dislodge it.

CHAPTER 47

Ta was set. He turned on his penlight and aimed it at the floor, and began his trek towards Jules. His gun was at the ready, gripped like a vise in his right hand. Closer he came. No one seemed to notice the masquerading usher moving through the aisle, probably to handle some insignificant issue. There was Jules, only a few feet away from him. The big fool was still sitting there beside her, none the wiser. He would love to shoot him, but it wasn't going to be today. He decided it wasn't worth the delay; his escape was the most important thing, and the sooner he could get moving back through the aisle, the cleaner his exit pathway. Ta covered the final steps, and then he was there. He positioned himself behind Jules and began to raise the pistol. But some kind of pressure on his right shoulder prevented any movement. Something slid around his neck, but he couldn't move to fight it. Seconds later, he blacked out.

CHAPTER 48

"Disguised himself." Those were Jules' words that nagged at my brain—that wouldn't come clear to me until just now. With the right disguise, Ta could get in here and move around freely. He could get close to Jules. But what would that disguise be? I scrutinize the theatre, looking for every possibility. A musician in the orchestra? They had already been playing for several minutes—someone would have noticed by now. Someone on stage? Again, too noticeable—he would have been blown by this point in the show. I look more and think harder. The ushers are all in uniform; could Ta get one of those?

Why not, I conclude. There are many ways he could obtain an ushers coat and hat. I send a quick text to Wan and wait. Less than a minute later, he is there. I whisper to Jules that I was going to check on something, and slip out of the loge. I explain to Wan that Ta may be disguised as an usher or in some other disguise. Wan takes my place beside Jules, armed and ready. I choose him for this task for a reason: of the members of the security force, he is the closest to my size; and he is incensed over the fact that Ta had put him in a position to have his loyalty questioned. I have no doubt that he will kill Ta without a moment's hesitation and never lose a wink of sleep over it.

I move from our aisle and towards the rear of the room. After a methodical assessment, I position myself where I can observe the aisles that lead to Jules' loge. I do so without creating a stir among the patrons, or blocking anyone's view. My vision is now fully acclimated to the dark, and I'm comfortable that I'll see what I need to. Minutes pass. I see the door to my right open, and an usher walks in. He starts down the aisle that runs behind our box, his penlight fixed on the floor. The audience is totally enthralled with the show—they don't even seem to be aware of the usher. His coat is different from the other ushers; you wouldn't notice it unless you were looking very closely, and I am. It has to be Ta or an accomplice. Nothing else around the theatre is suspicious, so I focus on this fake usher. I move down an aisle to my right and fall in close behind him; I have vowed not to take any chances with Jules' safety, so if I have to shoot him in this crowded theatre, then so be it. But we're not to that point—yet. Still no activity anywhere else in the theatre. A lone assassin. I see a pistol in his right hand, hanging to his side. He slows, his intentions obvious now: to move behind Jules and shoot her right there in the theatre. But I'm here, two feet behind him. I grasp the area where his shoulder meets his neck and clamp down—hard—while slipping my other arm around his neck. His arm goes hopelessly limp as the nerves rupture and sever in his trapezius, preventing any arm movement and causing dizziness and confusion—he can't move or think; he can do nothing. The pressure applied around his neck by my other arm finishes the job and puts him to sleep in seconds. The gun and light drop onto the carpeted floor, useless, creating some noise but causing no alarm, even though at this point, I don't care. I hook my hands under Ta's arms, catch him as his legs give way, as Wan turns and sees what's happening. I drag Ta through the aisle and out the door he entered. Once there, I pull some zip ties and a small roll of duct tape out of my suit coat pocket and secure his legs and hands, and tape his mouth. For good measure, I pull the zip ties plenty tight. He'll have some discomfort when he comes around. Maybe lose a limb or two because of poor circulation. But he'll live to face the music. Wan comes through the door, Princess in tow, Ta's pistol stuffed down the front of his pants.

Jules rushes to me and I get a well-deserved hug. For now, she believes I'm her hero.

Jules felt it necessary to return and see the entire opera; she was, after all, a guest of the First Lady. At the end of the show, they would cast spotlights on the dignitaries in attendance, and she wanted the King to know that she followed through with her commitment. If she missed the fanfare, he might hear about it. I send Wan back into the theatre with her.

I call the closest security man from his post. He had been watching a side entrance, which happened to be the closest door to where we were at the time.

I send him after a car and carry Ta out the side door. A real usher was watching us with some amazement, so I paid him off with a 100 Euro banknote. If anyone ever asks him, he's seen nothing. We load Ta into the trunk and my helper moves the car away from the door. I go back on duty, not taking any chances in case Ta has some type of back-up. If he did, we never saw or heard from them. The rest of the opera is bravissimo, the Princess glows under the spotlights for a moment, and we are off.

CHAPTER 49

Jules has such class. On the ride back, all she could talk about was how professional the opera players were, what great voices they had, how much she loved the orchestra. You would have never known that someone had just tried to kill her—again. And that 'someone' was duct taped in the trunk of a car.

When she finally gave it a rest, we talked about what we do from there.

I started. "I'd like to secure private transportation back to Muji if possible. I don't want to travel commercially with Ta unless I absolutely have to."

"I'll send for the King's jet. If he isn't using it, they'll come right away."

"Good. Have you thought about how you're going to work this with the King?"

She paused for a second. Whatever she was getting ready to say, it wasn't something she had 100% confidence in. "I've been thinking about that. I'm not sure I know the best way to do this. But in general, I think it's always best to be direct." Something I had already discovered about her. "Give him every fact and every suspicion. Let him filter it as he may. I remain convinced that his reaction will be the key."

"I can't disagree. You're looking for his reaction. Coming directly at him may catch him by surprise if he's trying to hide something. He's going to get the full story soon enough; might as well get it out there."

"That's where I'm at."

Back at the apartment, the security force made a quick check of the area, and we all unloaded. I walked to the back of the car with Jules and popped the trunk. Ta is not there.

Jules gasped. "Oh my God!"

I try to keep the joke going, but my grin betrays me. "He's in the other car."

"You have a twisted sense of humor. In fact, you're not funny at all."

We pop the trunk of the correct car, and there lays her nemesis, the cause of her pain, her asshole of a cousin. "Hello Ta. Comfy?" I couldn't help myself. The Princess stared at him with disdain and disappointment. She tries hard to see the best in everyone. Now that she fully comprehends, face to face, the evil that Ta truly is, it is difficult for her.

Fully conscious now, Ta grunts and struggles. He is feeling the pain of the zip ties. "You are a disgrace to Musjistan." That's how she sees it.

"I'm going to secure him with some other materials. He's an hour or so from permanent circulation problems." I pull him up out of the trunk, cut his legs free, and walk him into the apartment. His legs are shaky, but no one here seems to care.

I set him in a chair and cut the tape off his mouth. He breathes heavily, as if he had been holding his breath for the past two hours. "I don't know who you are, but you will not get away with this. I am on a mission from my King, and I will see you executed for this." He's invoked the King's involvement again. Hope it's just bravado.

"Oh, I have a feeling that someone's going to get executed, but I bet it isn't me."

"Fuck you. I will watch you die."

I stuff a dishcloth in his mouth and tape it shut again. "If that's the way you're going to be, maybe I'll just kill you now. Wouldn't have to worry about the King then, would I?"

I summon Wan to keep watch on Ta while I get some supplies out of my bedroom. When I come back, I affix a pair of wide zip ties to his wrists, get them to the correct tightness, and take out a lighter. I melt the ties a little on each side of the tab, not burning Ta enough to care. They're made not to get any looser, but they can tighten. I don't generally take the chance for either to happen. I repeat the procedure with two other wide ties. His hands secure, I cut off the old ties. I then do the same to his ankles. Double tied, top and bottom.

Jules came into the room, straight up angry, but under control as usual. "Ta, I always knew you were low. I knew you were jealous. I even knew you were stupid. But this? When this gets out, oh my God, the shame you will have brought on the Kingdom. And the pain you will bring to the King."

"Do you want him to answer or just want to deride him? I'm for just dogging him and not having to listen to his shit."

"Good enough for now. But sooner or later, I'm going to calm down enough to actually have a conversation."

That was a thought that needed some exploration. We should consider the best way to approach his interrogation.

I moved a chair next to a wrought iron security screening that was covering a window. I sat Ta in the chair. The window overlooked a fenced-in back yard, visible only from my apartment, so no one would see the fool. I grabbed a few more zip ties and slipped them through the ties on Ta's wrists and then attached them to the iron fixture. A steam pipe, normal for older buildings here, ran along the base of the wall under the window, and I ran a couple of more zip ties through the ones on Ta's ankles and secured them to the steam pipe. He wasn't going anywhere. I'll find a way to make him little more comfortable overnight, although I don't know why.

CHAPTER 50

Jules decided it was time to talk to Ta. It was late, but it was clear that she wasn't going to sleep until she questioned him.

"Let's go see Ta."

"It's late. He's sleeping."

"Like you care that he's sleeping. I want to get his story on record. I want him to tell us exactly how the King is involved. The more elaborate the details we can get him to provide, the better the chance he'll screw them up later. And if by some slim chance he's telling the truth, then maybe he can give us proof."

"Okay. You're the boss. Would you like me to impose some tried and true methods of achieving full disclosure?"

"No. And don't think I don't know what you mean."

"Just thought I would offer."

"Well, for now, no." A glimmer of hope. Might get to torture this scum after all.

In order to let him sleep, I had cut his hands loose from the wrought iron window grate and let him lay down. I zip tied his wrists to the same steam pipe his legs were secured to. He was sleeping when Jules and I came to talk.

"Any trouble from him?" I asked Sesia, who had taken first watch.

"Not a peep."

"Thanks. I'll take over. Why don't you go get some rest."

"Thanks." He turned to Jules and bent his head forward. "Majesty."

"Good night Sesia. Please try to rest."

She spoke directly to Ta, in a tone that a schoolteacher might employ when she had caught a student passing a note. "Ta, wake up."

He didn't budge, so I did my part and kicked him in the ribs. He was now officially awake.

Jules glared at me and I shrugged. "I'm going to ask my friend here to take off your gag. When he does, we will have a civil conversation about this whole mess. You will not yell, you will not be disrespectful, and you will answer my questions truthfully. I know the truth often escapes your intellect, but I assure you, my friend expects the truth, and will not be pleased if he doesn't get it." Now we're getting somewhere.

I remove the gag. Ta actually stays quiet.

"Now, what the hell?" Jules seemed to have gone a little off the reservation.

"I am working for the King. This is a mission directly from the Crown. The King ordered your death, and sent me to do it to prove my worthiness for the Throne. If anything happens to me, the King will avenge me. He already wants you gone, so doing anything to me will only hasten your ultimate doom."

"So if the King is behind this, when did he commission you to do this deed?"

"I will say nothing further. But if I don't return to Musjistan unharmed, the King will track you to the ends of the earth and you will both die a painful death."

"So you won't talk anymore, or you just don't have any more lies ready? The King has always thought you had a big mouth. He's said many times that you cannot be trusted. So keep talking asshole."

Ta was incensed. Jules' ploy was working, at least in that regard. But Ta held out. "I will tell you nothing. But I strongly recommend that you free me and find a very good hiding place. Your only chance to live is if the King never finds you."

"You of course know that I've already talked to the King? And he says you're lying scum and always have been."

"You lie. He would never say that about me."

"He would. And he did. 'Lying scum'. His exact words."

"Fuck you and your man-whore. You are no Princess. And you will never sit on the Throne of Musjistan. Unless you release me and disappear forever, you will die like the traitor you are." Man-whore? I think I'm flattered.

"I'm going to take my chances with the King. If he wants me dead, then he can make that happen when I take you to him."

"It's your funeral." Ta had made his stand. To my dismay, Jules prohibited my special brand of inducement, so that was all we were going to get from him.

Sesia's relief showed up about this time. Jules was exhausted. We decided to knock off for now and see what the morning would bring.

CHAPTER 51

Jules was melancholy. She wanted to talk. "I can't believe Ta went this far off the deep end. He can't think that I would ever believe the King is part of this."

"Yet you're thinking, 'what if he is?'" The elephant in the room.

"As much as I hate to admit it, listening to Ta does make me wonder a little. I still don't believe he could have anything to do with this, but it worries me that Ta is so adamant."

"What choice does he have? Either fess up to everything, or hope you'll believe the King is involved and drop off the face of the earth. Think about it. If the King is not involved, the only chance Ta has is for you believe that he is."

"That's a lot of ifs and buts."

"So it is. Maybe all for naught. But sometimes things end well. This could be one of those times."

"I love your optimism." She was breathing the slow deep breaths of sleep within minutes. My phone signaled an email. I had asked the SIC if they could give me anything on the King. And they were responding with a little bedtime story.

Less than two decades ago, Jules' grandfather became engaged in a controversial movement and, as a member of the Royal Family, he used his influence and access to further their ideology. He and his collaborators were pushing for the Country to convert their financial reserves to a gold standard and print their own currency, much like America, and leave the European Union. Their thinking was that the move would preserve the Kingdom's wealth and separate their economy from the rest of Europe. They believed that the European economy, and subsequently the Euro, would fail in the near future. The sitting Royalty and the political powers of Muji rejected the idea of leaving the European Union. They saw it as the failsafe for their security; with no military, the Country was defenseless without their European allies. The movement stalled, but not before Jules' grandfather had been publicly rebuked by the King. Jules' parents took a stand with the King in favor of staying with the Union. Only one member of the Royal Family supported Jules' grandpa: Ta's mother. When Jules' grandfather took the Throne years later, Ta, now an adult, made public statements about how he agreed with the idea of their own currency. A kiss-ass move for sure.

The Turks considered this information as a possible motive for the King to prefer Ta to Jules. I could understand the King wanting his successor to share his philosophies, but plotting an assassination to make that happen didn't ring true. Nonetheless, for the first time we had something other than Ta's rantings as a potential motive for the King.

I emailed the SIC again and asked them to keep digging. The reply was immediate: We're done digging. Now do your job and get the goods on Ta. They wanted no threat of instability when Jules became Queen.

Time to get some rest. I'll need it when I take this information to Jules tomorrow.

CHAPTER 52

We stayed the night at the apartment. Three security men were there as well, taking shifts watching Ta.

Jules woke early, and as soon as I sensed she was awake, I was awake too. That's kind of a thing for me. I can tell myself when to go to sleep and when to wake up, and my body listens. It's a handy gift. She snuggled up under my arm. "Buck, you never told me your last name."

"I don't have one."

"So you have one name. Like Madonna or Prince."

"More like Madonna and Zeus. Not like Prince. He changed his name to some one that used to be Prince, or something like that."

"Zeus only had one name?"

"I never heard another one. Have you?"

"No. But you are neither a pop singer nor a Greek god. So what's your last name, Buck?"

"Why do you want to know?"

She looked exasperated. "Are you joking? We're sleeping together nearly every night, we're in love or something like it, and you think I should have some grand reason other than that for wanting to know your last name?"

"When you put it like that..." She's making this hard. At the risk of scaring her away, I decide to be honest. "Look, if someone doesn't know something, it can't be tortured out of them, right?"

"Where is this going?"

"Just bear with me. This is important."

"Fine. You're correct. Information cannot be tortured out of someone if they don't know the information to start with."

"Right. So I make enemies in this line of work. On a routine basis. Life-long enemies, some of whom would do or pay anything to find me and kill me. I know that sounds dramatic, but that's the way it is."

"And?"

"And...everyone who deals with me, or has ever dealt with me, or ever will deal with me, knows that I have one firm, absolutely non-negotiable, hard and fast rule: I never tell anyone my full name or where I live. I get contacted through a secure dark website and a super-duper secret squirrel encrypted email account. I can never be traced electronically, and there will never be anyone who knows where I live or who I am."

"So nobody will ever be tortured to provide information about you. Is that it?"

"Yep. And if anybody ever is, I will know about it. And then I would kill whoever tortured them—that's also a rule of mine. So not only would they never find me, but they would die for their efforts."

"I'm supposed to believe that?"

"Nope. Believe what you want. Your choice. But it's my choice not to tell anyone my name."

"Glad we cleared that up. But I promise, we'll have this conversation again someday. Want to get breakfast and take another run at Ta?"

"Breakfast it is. But I got some information last night that you need to hear." So I told her what the Turks sent me and how it maybe could be a motive for the King to plan her demise.

"I'm not buying it, but I will tell you, the doubt has been planted."

"I'm sorry to be the one to tell you."

"Don't worry about that. You're a cute messenger."

"Cute? After all we've been through together? How about 'dashing' or 'handsome'?"

"Let me think about it."

Relegated to 'cute'. "I'll make us some eggs."

CHAPTER 53

I tried to discourage Jules from talking with Ta again. She didn't need to hear all the hate and vitriol that came out of his ignorant head. And I didn't believe he would give her anything more or change his story. But she wanted to try, so we did.

Ta stuck to his story. So we tried Mistaf again, and he had nothing else to offer. This brought Jules to the point where she needed to wrap things up in Greece and get home; just get on with it. Confront the King and figure out where she stands.

She called for the private jet and scheduled the flight back for the next morning. The jet would fly in tonight, the crew would layover on the mainland, and we would meet them at the airport tomorrow for the big bon voyage.

While her aides were busy packing up the condo, Jules came back to the apartment that afternoon to help me clear the place out. When she got there, my go bag and duffle were packed and sitting by the bed.

"I see you have a couple of your bags packed. What can I help with?"

"My toothbrush, I guess? Everything else is packed."

"You've been here for a month. You have two bags?"

"I travel light, you know."

"Light doesn't begin to explain this. Two small bags? Anyway, I would like to be on the tarmac by 8 tomorrow morning. Is that going to be a problem?"

"Not for me. I picked up a couple of body bags from the local morgue for Ta and Mistaf. They'll be traveling in comfort."

"Seriously, how are we going to manage them during the trip?"

"I've assigned a full three-man security team to each of them. They will be restrained the entire time, and will be seated as far forward as possible on the flight. If they don't behave, I'll gag and hog-tie them. The guys have been fully briefed."

"I'm not worried. Anything weird comes up, I know you'll handle it."

"You know, it's not the best of ideas for me to be traveling with you. I'm confident that I'm under the radar, but the fact is, I have stayed here too long. There's no evidence that I've been tracked, and nothing to bring the SIC under suspicion, but the most cautious option would be for me to travel separately. I think it could be safer for you."

"But we have no other threat right now?"

"Not to you. But if the Turks somehow got careless and information about me was siphoned from them, then I could attract some trouble."

"But you just said you have no reason to believe that SIC has been compromised."

"Absolutely none. But if it were me, and I intercepted info from the Turks, I would be sure that no one knew I had accessed their system. So what do we really know?"

"I think we know you're paranoid…"

"Perhaps. But it keeps me alive."

"Well I think you should travel with me unless there is some indication of a threat to you."

"Fair enough. Just wanted you to know the risk."

I made sure that Ta and Mistaf got scrubbed down for the journey. Didn't want them stinking up the jet. We had searched them thoroughly when we got them here, but a bath was insurance against anything that might have been missed. I explained to the security force how to do it, making certain that their hands and legs were never free at the same time, and that two of our team had to be present at all times during the cleansing. I would sanitize the apartment in the morning after everyone was out, leaving no trace of my presence. I had a spray bottle of some stuff I scored in Tokyo—a mist that instantly compromised prints, DNA, hair, anything it landed on. I could eradicate the apartment of any proof of my existence within minutes. I wanted to do the same with the condo, but knew my opportunity for that would be limited. I had exercised caution there anyway—didn't touch anything I didn't absolutely have to, and wiped down what I had. I was careful not to be too obvious, but I didn't really care if anyone saw. I was basically exposed by the events that unfolded after the assassination plot was foiled.

The two prisoners would be restrained the entire trip. Zip ties would be added between their leg restraints to form makeshift leg chains. They would be able to shuffle, but not run.

That evening, I personally briefed Ta about his behavior on the trip. "We're going on a little trip soon. I don't care if you live through it or not. Were I you, I would consider that before doing anything stupid. You follow?"

He resented me talking to him at all, but he nodded.

"During this trip, I don't plan to gag you. But that will change the second you start running your mouth. Anything comes out of your pie hole that the Princess, the security force, the aides, or I don't like, then I'll gag you for the remainder of the trip and possibly all eternity. Dig?"

He nodded again.

"I'll let you know when you can relieve yourself. If you don't like my schedule, you can piss in your pants. I don't care. We'll feed you enough to keep you alive—again, on my schedule. If the security men tell you to do something, you do it. Period. Follow these simple rules, and you just might live another day."

Ta wanted the final say. "You think you are so fucking smart. You think that because these fools follow you, the King will believe anything you say. You are sadly mistaken. I will watch you die, and will watch your precious Princess die. And I'll enjoy it. You are playing right into my hands."

"I wonder Ta, why would you tell me we're playing into your hands? Wouldn't you rather just keep us in the dark and relish the surprise when we find out the King is with you?"

"Jules is family. She is stupid and immature, but I no longer wish her dead. I would rather she just fled and lived, so I say these things to convince her of her fate, and maybe save her life."

"So, out of the goodness of your heart, you changed your mind?" It was rhetorical, and I didn't give him a chance to answer. All of a sudden, he wants to save Jules from death? Maybe a self-inflicted hole in his story out of desperation to get me to believe him. No matter. We would soon know the truth. I stuffed a rag into his mouth and wrapped some fresh duct tape around his head. Wish I could get odds on how long he'll make it tomorrow before he gets gagged.

CHAPTER 54

I had the security guys take several of the vehicles back to the rental place that evening. I wanted four vehicles to make the trip to the airport, and I needed a full complement of security in each of them. When the guys got back from the airport, we met for our evening briefing.

"Gentlemen, this is the last chance to prepare for tomorrow's trip. There is no evidence of any threat. We will of course act as if there is. We have retained four of the big rental SUVs for the trip to the airport. Ta will be in the second vehicle with four of you. Mistaf will be in the third vehicle with another four. Two of you will be assigned as drivers for the other vehicles, and the remainder will be spread out between those vehicles. I will ride in the lead vehicle with the Princess. Normally I wouldn't put her in the lead vehicle, but with the prisoners, it is either the lead or the trail, and the lead lends itself to more support from you all, should something go bad. The aides will be in the chase vehicle. Stay in tight formation; if the lead vehicle goes through an intersection, we all do. If we get ambushed, the priority is the Princess. Rally to her vehicle. When we get to the tarmac, I will give the all clear when it's safe to unload. Any comments, suggestions, questions?" A silent room. Real pros. "Good. Sesia and Wan have your assignments. See them right after this. Thanks."

Later on, Jules and I had a chance to visit for a spell. She was pensive and focused. "So this is it. Tomorrow we travel to Muji and put it all on the line."

"Yep. The guys are ready. Ta and Mistaf shouldn't cause any problems. You and I will ride together to the airport. Is the condo crew all packed?"

"The aides were just about finished when I left. Not really much of a job. A little more than yours though." She smiled a little, maybe feeling a little less anxiety.

"You alright?"

"Yes. This is stressful, you know. So much at stake. I want to have faith in the King. But I don't want to be blinded by it."

"I don't think you are. You're just considering all the information that you have. It is, at least in part, inconclusive. So it's natural for your mind to let all eventualities have a place. It doesn't make you disloyal. Just means you're smart."

"I'm going to try to get some rest. You coming in?"

"In just a few."

I did a final check of the apartment, outside and in. Nothing stood out. The area around the apartment was quiet. I hadn't had much in the way of neighbors my entire stay—it was off-season for the island. The apartments were each on separate lots, more like villas.

Mine was the last one, on the far edges of the property. Even though there for work, the first part of my stay had rendered a nice little vacation.

I listened intently to the night. I could hear the businesses down the hill. Restaurants and bars mostly. To the east, I could hear the surf; just barely. I blocked out those sounds and focused on the west. Primarily residential up there. Some low voices, and an occasional laugh. Weird, but I had always enjoyed just listening to the things around me.

Back in the apartment, I peeked in on Sesia. He had Ta under watch. "Everything good? You need a little break?"

"All good here. Don't need a thing. I'll get relieved in 20."

"Okay. I'm turning in. You know where I am if you need anything."

"Sure do. Get some rest."

"See you tomorrow."

I lay in bed, going through contingencies in my mind. If the King was on the other side, I would be forced to fight for Jules. Alone. The men with me now wouldn't likely stand against their King. Me against all the King's men, so to speak. Not great odds. I couldn't plan specifics, because the castle, or whatever the King lived in, was unknown territory to me. But what is known is that I will do anything to ensure Jules' safety.

CHAPTER 55

Jules roused at about 6. I had been up for a couple of hours. She had been very restless, so I couldn't sleep. I finally got up in hopes that she might rest better with the whole bed to herself. She found me in the kitchen. "You got coffee?"

"Of course. Coming up. A little cream, just how you like it."

I was dressed and my bags were at my feet. "You're ready to go?"

"Yes Boss. Been ready for about 90 minutes."

"I'll be ready in a half hour."

"No hurry. We're good on time."

We were pulling out of the condo 45 minutes later. The trip to the ferry took about ten minutes. We timed it well and only had to wait about five minutes before they started loading. On the boat, four of the security men posted at each corner of our block of vehicles. The ride went fast. We pulled off onto the mainland and motored on to the airport.

The tarmac was clean—no other private jets loading or unloading at the time. The security force met briefly with the flight crew and confirmed that they were who they were supposed to be. While everyone was loading up, I inspected the exterior of the jet with the pilot and saw nothing unusual. The co-pilot came back and gave a short welcome and the nickel version of the safety briefing, and minutes later we were airborne. Jules and I settled in. Nothing left to say. Five hours to touchdown in Muji.

I checked out the ride. It comfortably seated about 30. The galley could feed a small country. I guess, in a way it did. The lone flight attendant stayed busy and kept everyone happy. Except Ta and Mistaf, I presume. She served a meal, chicken and a nice sauce with asparagus and a salad. Those that didn't want a full meal were treated to a selection of sandwiches. I went for the chicken, and loved it. Then a bourbon to settle the food.

CHAPTER 56

The Kingdom had a private landing strip. The ground crew ushered the plane into a huge hangar and the steps rolled up to the door. I had no idea what to expect. This was the first of possibly many threat situations, so I'm on edge. What has the King been told? Jules swears she's told him nothing—going for the element of surprise. But she summoned six additional security men and the private jet, so even if the King doesn't know details, certainly he suspects something is up.

Turns out, there wasn't anything to expect. No one on the ground but the crew from the hangar. The security guys led the way down the steps, Ta and Mistaf in tow, Jules following with her escorts. I took up the rear, not wanting any more attention than necessary. Limos pulled up to the hangar door. The security force checked them out carefully, while I stood guard by Jules. Nothing suspicious, so the luggage was loaded, and seconds later we were exiting the airfield. Not more than a few words were exchanged, and they were mostly "Welcome home Princess." That kind of thing.

The trip from the airport took less than 15 minutes. We pulled through an archway and parked in a courtyard. The Palace was impressive. Suitable for any ruler. With a footprint larger than an acre, it rose three stories out of the landscape with wings on each side, each about half the size of the center structure. Marble, bath stone, and bronze topped the list of building materials on the exterior. Nice. I stood outside the limo for a minute, checking out what I could see. No visible threats. "You can come out now Jules."

"Don't you think by now it's a little late to worry about an ambush? We're in the lair. Trust the outcome."

"Sorry, can't do that."

We walked to the nearest double-doors. Big enough to drive a truck through, but well-fortified. Four uniformed soldier-looking dudes met us there—the Palace Guard. Jules had recommended that they secure Ta and Mistaf. She was comfortable that they could not be corrupted. I wasn't comfortable that they wouldn't kill us if so ordered. Their legacy in Muji was legendary—extremely regimented, committed to the Unit for their entire career, sworn to secrecy their entire life. Lived and worked together; no distractions. Sounded a lot like the Old Guard in D.C. They took possession of Ta and Mistaf and escorted them to the Palace confinement quarters—a nice term for jail.

The interior of the palace was no less impressive than the outside. Ornate, as expected, and absolutely laid out. I'd been in a palace or two in my lifetime, and never saw a bad one, but this was up there with the best. Jules took us to a parlor of some kind and called the First Advisor to the King. She asked if we could see him. Anytime, he said. The King must be anxious to see his granddaughter.

"You must be in a hurry. I haven't even set my bags down."

"No reason to put it off. Leave any weapons here. Not good form to show up armed to a meeting with the King." I didn't like the sound of that. But this was her show, and nothing had alarmed my senses yet.

"Will your security team be armed?"

"Always."

"But they would shoot me if the King told them to?"

"Of course."

"Nice hospitality. Give me a second to hide it somewhere." An ornate table with a drawer was about the only available storage, so that's where the Glock and Leatherman went. "Okay. Let's do this."

CHAPTER 57

The Princess played tour guide on our way. Pointed out paintings and explained how rooms got their names—that kind of thing. She was acting as if this were just another day at the palace. But I could tell that her anxiety festered just beneath the surface. As tough as she was, she couldn't hide it.

We entered a large board room. There were guards, dressed like the gentlemen that whisked Ta and Mistaf away, in every corner and at every door. Three other guys were seated near the far end of a huge table. Seated at the head was an older statesman, who looked very much like he could be a king. Jules went quickly to his side. He rose out of his chair and they embraced. Not a word was spoken. I took that as a good sign. Jules backed away. "Majesty, you look well."

"I fear from what I have heard thus far today that soon enough I won't be feeling so well."

"Sorry to bring you bad news, grandfather, but we have had quite an ordeal. I'm afraid we must ask you to intervene."

"And who is your friend?" I was instructed not to speak unless spoken to.

"Your Highness, this man saved my life. His name is Buck. He was on holiday on the same island as I when the problems began."

"I see" he said softly to her. Then he looked over at me. "You saved my granddaughter's life, did you? Do you understand the honor that bestows upon you?"

"Uh, Sir. The Princess makes more of this than it warrants. I was involved, yes. And I am very relieved that it all worked out. I wish for nothing in return but that you hear her story and maybe calm her anxiety."

"Modesty. I see." Back to her: "Jules, please sit down and tell me everything."

"In fairness, perhaps Ta and Mistaf should be here?"

"I have been told that they now take residence in the confinement quarters. But you want them here?"

"I think it best, Majesty."

"Fine." He waved to a guard and the guard leaned into his ear. After a second, "The Chief of the Guard has them waiting just outside. Why don't we show them in?"

"Yes my King, I advised the Guard that they may be needed here."

"Very well." Ta and Mistaf were brought in. Mistaf looked pale; even frightened. Ta stared defiantly at Jules, but acquiesced with a low nod to the King.

"Now, Jules, since you are one *not* in handcuffs, please go ahead."

"Majesty, when I was in Greece, I ran into Buck. We became friends. Information came to him that a plot to assassinate me was afoot. Sources of Buck's, very good sources, had intercepted communications from Ta about purchasing weaponry to launch an attack. The attack was to appear as a terrorist attack against Greece. I was to be killed in this attack. Ta was never to become under suspicion because I would have been collateral damage; not the target. When the attack was stopped by Buck, Ta went on the run in Greece, and Buck caught him in the act of trying to shoot me in the back of the head as I watched the Russian Opera. There are many more details, but most important are these two: During interrogation, Mistaf stated that Ta indicated that the King—you, Your Excellency—knew about the plan to kill me." The King had no change of emotion whatsoever. "When Ta was captured, he told us that you ordered my death to keep me from the Throne. And now, here we are."

The King was stoic. He let Jules' narrative marinate for a moment, then turned to Ta. "Ta? Do you have a side to this incredible story?"

"Your Highness, may we please meet alone? This is quite sensitive as you know."

"We may not. Say what you have to say."

"Well, I have sensed your dissatisfaction with the intentions of the Princess. We have discussed how she plans on throwing the wealth of the Crown away. This Country has thrived because of the hard-working citizenry and because our Rulers have protected our wealth over the years. You fear the damage she could do to the Kingdom if in control of the purse strings, as do I. I understood your frustration and made the next bold step to eradicate such a threat. You may have not been specific with the order, but I knew what you wanted. I urge you now to finish what I have started. Banish Jules. Designate me as your successor. I will rule as you have ruled."

"And when exactly did I say these things that meant I wanted Jules dead?"

"During our time together—our various meetings."

"Just name one specific meeting, Ta. Just one. Where and when?"

Ta was thinking, but it looked like the King had him trapped somehow. "Let me help you with that, Ta." The King turned towards his advisors at the table. "Sitting here are my advisors. One of their jobs is to record my every movement outside of the Palace. Gentlemen, is there any record of a meeting outside of the Palace with Ta? And do not mask the truth—be completely forthcoming, I insist."

One of the advisors to the King's left had a large ledger. He patted it calmly. "No need to check the register, Your Majesty. Such a meeting has never occurred—there were none. Only social gatherings where no business meetings can be convened. That is your edict unless an official meeting is scheduled."

"Ta, do you allege that I met with you somewhere outside the Palace for this discussion?"

"No Your Majesty. I have only met with you here at the Palace."

"Then again, I must ask, when? And what words exactly did I use that would give you the idea that I wanted Jules dead?" The discomfort clung to Ta like a flea to a dog.

"Your Majesty, the exact date escapes me."

"Fine. The exact words then. Surely something as important as an order for the death of a Crown Princess left nothing to chance, right?"

"I know what I understood you to say."

"So you say. Who else heard this conversation; this death wish I put on Jules?"

"No one Majesty. We were alone." I thought a hint of a smile formed on Jules' lips.

"Advisors, please check the record and see when I met with Ta alone?"

"You did not, Your Majesty."

"You know without checking?"

"Everyone in the palace knows that you have never met with anyone completely alone. An advisor or other confidant is always present at your meetings. You decreed this when you first became King." That explained the little smile from Jules.

"And why would I do such a thing?"

The First Advisor stood and faced Ta. And he did not look happy. "I imagine Majesty, because of situations like this: When someone makes an allegation that could otherwise not be disproven; that is, not without a witness."

The King paced around the end of the table, looking thoughtful, but not distressed. He looked from Mistaf, to Ta, to Jules, and then to me, and then in a stern voice proclaimed: "Ta, you have been proven a liar here today. And I suppose some in this room may believe that my lovely granddaughter here is questioning my honor." His gaze came to rest on Jules, and his tone softened. "But those with an actual working brain know that you are not questioning my honor. You gave me facts and gauged my reaction." He winked at Jules. "It's what I would do in your situation.

"You chose not to run. I would hope that I would not have run either. Even if Ta had been telling the truth, it would be better to stand in the face of a corrupt King and be sentenced, than to flee my Country without trying to restore honor to the Throne. Jules, I count this as a very noble and brave act on your part. I commend you. You, my dear, will be a great Ruler.

"Ta, other plans await you. I will consider your fate. Guards, take him."

Jules and the King sat to visit more, and I attempted to excuse myself.

"Nonsense" the King exclaimed. "You will sit with us and help Jules tell this fantastic story."

So I did. We gave every detail, even told him about the Turks. The King had no interest in exposing them; he just wanted to know everything. After it was all out, he sat back, shook his head, and looked at me. "Musjistan owes you everything. You literally saved Her Queen. You saved Her reputation. We are forever in your debt."

Not bad for a college dropout, huh?

CHAPTER 58

In the room now was the King, his First Advisor, Jules, and me. "I'm so relieved that you are okay, Jules. I hate that you went through this."

"I'm fine grandfather, thanks to Buck."

"Yes, we'll get to him soon. Jules, the manner by which you have comported yourself during this ordeal is nothing less than Royal. I am old; frankly, weary. The business of the Crown is constant. And you have shown Yourself to be worthy in every way. So I'm going to step back from some things before I begin faltering under the weight. Today, I am elevating your role in the Kingdom. With the counsel of my advisors, and any others you chose yourself, many decisions will become yours to make. We'll meet soon and determine exactly how the responsibilities of the Crown will be divided—what will be yours, and what will be mine. But for now, know that you have my full trust and confidence. And since we have not agreed on all matters financial when it comes to the wealth of Musjistan, consider this your chance to sway my thinking."

"Grandfather, this is sudden. I'm not ready for this. I have so much to learn."

"And wouldn't you rather learn while I am here to guide you?"

"Yes, most definitely. It offers me such an advantage."

"You will soon learn what it takes to keep this Country operating smoothly, both in terms of finances and governing. Once you do, I have faith that all your decisions, financial and otherwise, will be in the best interest of the Kingdom and her citizens. I won't take no for an answer, Princess Jules. I need you; your Country needs you." He laid a hand on her shoulder. "For the good of Musjistan, we must do this together."

Jules looked pensive. "Yes grandfather. I will do as you wish."

"And be considering how you will further the lineage. You need an heir." He smiled at her.

"That's the furthest thing from my mind."

"It shouldn't be. You are the last of the family that has any real connection to the Throne. All others are distantly related and their bloodline can be challenged by the politicians. The very fabric of the Kingdom would be threatened if they take over."

That she knew to be true. "I'll consider that, Majesty."

The King turned to me. "And you, Sir. The Kingdom owes you a debt that can never be fully repaid. How can I repay you?"

"That won't be necessary."

"A choice that is not yours. If you have no desires, then I will bequeath what I deem fitting. For starters, you will be awarded Musjistan's highest honor: The King's Medal of Valor. You will be the toast of Musjistan. You'll never pay for another meal or another stitch of clothing. A home and a full household staff will be provided for you. You will want for nothing. All that the Kingdom has to offer will be yours for the asking."

"Sir, may I speak freely?"

"Of course. All heroes may." He smiled. He was making me feel pretty good.

"Your gratitude is humbling. Understand that I did nothing more than I should have; nothing that you would not have done to save your granddaughter. But such attention is not possible. I can't be specific about it, but my work comes with many hazards. The publicity you speak of would bring danger to your Country. Many bad people want me dead—some of them quite powerful. When they find out I'm here—and they will—they will stop at nothing to destroy me, and that will likely be at the expense of Muji. So I'm sorry, but please understand, there can be no fanfare; no celebration; no public awards. It must be this way."

The King looked at Jules. She spoke. "Grandfather, I have known Buck for only a short time. But I vouch for him in every way. If he says he fears for the safety of Muji, it is real. You're looking at a man who fears nothing and no man. His worry is for Muji; not for himself. We must honor his request." Smart. She turned my demand into a request—easier for a King to accept.

"So be it. Your first official decision." He smiled at Jules. Looking back at me, he asked, "What are your immediate intentions? Will you stay here, live here? You can do so in privacy. You have my guarantee on that."

"I'll be around for a little while." I didn't have other plans right now.

CHAPTER 59

Confinement quarters. In Ta's case, death row. The King wasted no time. He sentenced Ta to death the very next day, and the execution was set for just a few hours afterwards. They didn't mess around in Muji.

Ta sat in his room. A very secure room, as it were. Mistaf got off easy, Ta thought. The King blamed Ta for much of Mistaf's actions, because he was Ta's servant. His official title was "assistant", but anyone who knew Ta understood that working for him was pure servitude. So the King banished Mistaf from civilization; exiled, you could say. He was soon going to be taken on a one-way trip to a desolate outpost in central Muji, where he would finish out his days in a work camp.

Ta was not dejected, as one might expect. He waited, feeling certain that the King would come to his senses. He reflected on his greed, his anger, and his predicament. Even now, it didn't occur to him to be remorseful. Musjistan should have been his. That was the only acceptable end.

"Ta". Jules voice, coming through the small port in the door. "Ta, get up please. Come speak to me."

"Speak to you? You are the reason I am here. Why would I speak to you?"

"You should know that I did not want this for you. I asked the King for mercy, to just send you away with Mistaf."

"You asked the King for mercy, did you? For me? Sure you did."

"Ta, I can't help what you believe, but the truth is that I asked him to spare your life. You should know that."

"And you should know that you were lucky. Were it not for weak, stupid people like Mistaf, you would be as dead as your foolish parents. My time is not over. You will pay when I get out of here. Now leave me."

"Ta, there is nothing more to be done. The King is resolute." Jules paused, waiting for some sign of repentance. Nothing. "I'll go now. May God have mercy on you."

"And may the devil dance on your grave you bitch! And that right soon!" The last words he ever spoke to Royalty.

Soon, the door opened, and Ta's aggression escalated, and suddenly fear entered the equation as his situation became real to him. The Palace Guards were all business. Ta resisted the restraints, but to no avail. He was shackled and had to be dragged, yelling obscenities until he reached the execution chamber, at which point his yells changed to sobs. He cursed and whined and begged, but the guards were unaffected. Minutes later, he was hanged like the common criminal he made himself into.

The Chief of the Guard slipped silently into the Parlor where the King was meeting with his Council. He was there only a moment when he caught the King's eye, and rendered an almost imperceptible nod. No acknowledgement needed, the King returned to his guests while the Chief left as silently as he entered. Ta was gone, his debt paid.

CHAPTER 60

The King assigned me an opulent room on the other side of the palace from Jules. Intentional no doubt. Probably felt like she didn't need the distraction.

I took out the cabinet-shelf nano and checked the website. The Iraq job had come back up. Apparently that problem wasn't solved. There was another job—almost domestic. Canada. It looked profitable and boring. I could go for that right now. And a South American human trafficking deal—I would almost do those for free. I made no decisions. I answered them all as "under consideration". That often increased the offer, although that wasn't my intent today. I just didn't know what I wanted to do.

To the King's credit, Ta was dispatched quickly. Mistaf got a break because he was somewhat forced to do Ta's bidding. He was sentenced to a work camp in the middle of nowhere, never to be seen by free people again. Real justice in both cases. Don't see much of that these days.

My time at the palace ran into weeks. Without actually making a decision, it was evident that I wasn't ready to move on just yet. Jules and I were spending some quality time together. Even though she was busy, we finally had an environment wherein the relationship could flourish. No one was trying to kill her, and I had nothing important to do. When she was working, I spent my time helping around the palace. I worked with the gardener, the security force, the stable hands—anyone who needed a little help. Even tried helping the chef one day, but he put a quick stop to that when my lack of culinary talent was exposed.

Sometimes Jules would dress me up and take me to some function. I was the good escort, tending to her needs, fetching drinks, whatever. Always introduced as her 'friend'. I enjoyed watching her. Despite her hesitation to take on all this responsibility, it suited her. She had found her niche'.

Jules and I usually dined with the King, and then would occupy ourselves with different things. We spent many evenings roaming the Royal city. Jules was educating me on all things Muji. Sometimes we would go dancing. Sometimes we would take a moonlight cruise on the Sea. Must admit, it was all kind of fun. As was being in a mature adult relationship. In other times, I could go months without meaningful and honest human contact. I was liking this. No matter how this ended, I knew it never truly would. This was one of those relationships that years later could pick up just where it left off. Don't get many of those. Maybe one or two in a lifetime.

I was working in the stables one afternoon when Jules came to find me in the barn. "Hey" I said. Her look warned me of a serious discussion coming my way.

"Hi. Can we talk a minute?"

"Sure." We walked out of the barn into the fresher air outside. "Everything okay?"

"Well, I'm not sure. Kind of depends on you."

"What is it Jules? Beating around the bush doesn't suit you."

"I know. But this is very difficult." She thought a minute and continued. "When we first met, I had not been in a relationship with man for a long time. You caught me by surprise. The attraction was real from the start, and somehow I knew we could have something special."

"Good. That's how it was for me."

"But because I hadn't been with anyone for so long, I wasn't prepared."

"Same for me. I never saw it coming."

"But it's more than that for me. I wasn't prepared in *any* way." She was really struggling with something. "And I need to tell you…well…"

"Come on Jules. You know you can tell me anything."

"I'm pregnant." She blurted.

Oh boy. Wow. One of the rare times in the history of me that I was speechless.

"The first couple of times we were, umm, together, I hadn't yet been able to get pills. But I did so as soon as I could. The day after our first time, I put one of my aides on a mission to find some, and she did. But it was about three days later. We had slept together a couple of times by then. I'm sorry, I know I shouldn't have done it without the pills. But I wasn't worried. It wasn't some childish impatience, believe me. There was just no concern, no worry that it could ever turn out bad. So I went with it. I can't explain." She looked up at me. "I couldn't stand for you to hate me. Say something. Please."

I tried to compose myself. I finally said the only thing that came to mind. "I love you, Jules. How's that for something?" She hugged me. Hard.

What ensued was a lengthy conversation about how she would handle this, what we each needed out of life, where we saw ourselves in nine months, about everything that you could expect would be discussed after a bombshell like this one landed on you. Decisions had to be made.

"Jules, whatever you think, I won't abandon you. But things have to be a certain way. No one in my world can ever, ever think I have a child. He or she would never be safe if it was known I was the father." I tingled a bit when saying "she"; a pure, sweet, little princess, growing up to be like Jules. What a rush.

"The child would be under the protection of the Crown."

"And unfortunately, I have enemies who wouldn't give that a second thought. They respect nothing. We can't take the chance. I haven't thought this completely through, but the bottom line is this: No one can know that I have a child. That being said, if you'll have me, I will never abandon you or the child. We just have to figure out what it will all look like."

So we talked about it. Expressed our thoughts out loud, bounced ideas and scenarios around. Tried to cover every eventuality, using the baseline premise that the safety of the child was primary, above all else. A child's life and a Queen's future hung in the balance. The decisions made now could impact Musjistan for generations to come.

Jules sent word that we wouldn't be joining the King for supper. We retreated to my room and, lacking energy for more talk, just existed together for a while.

CHAPTER 61

Jules made it clear: all decisions regarding the baby would be joint. She felt like our priorities were the same, and that we each understood the impact all this would have on the future of Muji. On this point, we were a unified front. And from that position of unity, the plan came together.

I would go away for a while. My presence gave rise to more suspicion than was worth risking. If I was not in the picture, Jules could explain away the pregnancy in a number of ways. In this day and age, artificial insemination was popular when a lineage was in need of heirs. And it maintained the purity of the bloodline, due to the anonymous nature of the donor process—nothing to muddy the waters, as it were. In fact, Jules had decided that, when the time was right, she would leak the story that she had been provided dozens of specimens that met strict criteria, selected from sperm banks around the Country. But only she knew which exact one had been chosen. The laws protecting the Royal Family would preclude any inquiry.

I could visit on occasion, but my visits needed to remain quiet and inconspicuous. I was no more than a friend to the King and his family. When Jules ascended to the Throne, it would only be natural that I stay connected to the King's family.

The child would never know I was the father. This part tugged at me in a place deep within that I didn't know even existed. I knew it to be the best thing. And I also knew that it would be painful.

Jules decided that the King should know. Their trust must be absolute. So we went to see him.

As normal, the King brought us in immediately. Upon request from Jules, the King excused his advisors. Like Jules, he believed in their mutual trust.

"Grandfather, the news I bring to you today is difficult to discuss. Buck is here because he is involved."

"And how long have you known about the baby?" he asked. Jules' mouth dropped open. I almost fell off my chair. "You expected less from a father and grandfather? I have seen many women in your condition. It's recognizable."

Jules recovered. "So you know? That relieves me of the fear of telling you."

"Yes, I have been suspicious for a week or so. You coming to me today and asking for the advisors to leave confirmed it. And you should never fear telling me anything that is the truth."

"Thank you, grandfather. And your feelings about this?"

"I couldn't be happier. You know the lineage has nearly run its course. This is exceptionally good news for Musjistan."

"I'm so glad to hear that. We have some plans, but we need for you to hear everything and lend your wisdom."

"It's good that you chose to confide in me. I'm excited that you will give us another heir. Are you happy?"

"Yes. We both are. But this has to be handled delicately, for the safety of the child. You see, Buck has enemies that would seek to do harm to anyone he is related to."

I stepped in. "Your Majesty, the motives would mainly be either revenge or to locate me. Some of these enemies have unlimited resources, both legal and underground. Some of them can get help from Interpol, Hamas, the CIA. Just about any intelligence agency or terrorist organization in the world. Every intelligence agency is compromised at some level. And among my enemies are those that have caused these compromises. Many are terrorists or do business with terrorists. Without going into any more detail, please accept that the child cannot be connected to me. It's not safe."

"You are not a bad person, Buck. Why would so many hate you so deeply? I'm sure you know that my security force had to make inquiries about you, as closely associated as you are with the Princess. The inquiries have come up empty. You are a ghost. But a ghost that I trust. You have proven yourself."

If you can't trust a King, who can you trust? So I give him more. "I am an operative that does work that government agencies cannot perform. You are a worldly person. I'm certain you understand what that must mean."

"Unfortunately, I do. Not every problem can be resolved through official channels."

"This work has taken me all over the world. While I'm personally known by very few, my persona is well known in many places, and by many bad people. And let me be crystal clear—I only work for good guys, and I never, ever hurt innocents. My missions are about maintaining peace; upholding law and order in the world."

"As you say."

"In short, I can't stay here. I must leave soon, and will not be able to come back for some time."

"You must realize that you have the discretion of the Crown? And we know how to keep secrets. Why would you not stay?"

"I fully understand, and I trust my secrets with you. But any minor slip-up could endanger Jules and the child. Every person that sees me becomes a potential target for information—which could mean torture and death. There are some who would torture innocent palace staff just to find me. I would like to believe that my identity has been protected here. But I have worries already. Some of your security force has some idea of what I do; I worked hand-in-hand with them in Greece. I trust them all, but under torture, eventually everyone talks. I know this to be true. I never want to be responsible for any harm coming to you, your family, your staff, or your citizens. So I must go away for a time. The baby must be born without me here, and I can't return until we are sure no one suspects I am the father."

"This brings me sadness. When I thought of the Princess being pregnant, the next thought was how good it would be to have you around permanently. I've grown very fond of you, and I see how much you mean to Jules. Parting company with you will be difficult."

"And for me. You have made me feel very much at home here. You are a man of wisdom and grace. This Country is extremely fortunate to have you on their Throne. I respect you enormously and will always admire you. How you handled the situation with Jules and Ta showed real character and leadership. Jules could have no one better to learn from."

"You flatter me, my friend. I will support whatever it is you must do. How may I assist?"

"I need passage out of the Country, and I would prefer not to have to cross any of your neighboring borders. Borders always get the most attention in the intelligence community. So, if not asking too much, could I maybe take a trip on your jet? I'll pay for the fuel and the crew."

"You'll do no such thing. In fact, I want to give you money to help ease your travels."

"Thank you, I'll accept the ride. However, I cannot accept any money. For one thing, I have plenty of money. My work pays well because my services are considered rare. And for another, I cannot take money for being here with Jules. She has enriched my life as money never could. This child will enrich my life even more. I appreciate the offer, but I would much prefer you know that I asked for nothing from you but the protection of Jules and our child, and your love for them as their grandfather."

"And that they shall have."

Jules' turn. "We will deflect the details of my pregnancy. I will leak information that will prevent the baby being traced to any man; basically, insemination. When the time comes, the child will be told the same story. So that's the plan. What is your counsel?"

"We must consider all eventualities so I have to ask this question—and don't just react. Think it through. Jules, have you considered that there may be another man in your future?"

"I hate to say this, because Buck and I have not talked about it. But yes, I understand that a Crown Princess may have many prospective suitors. There will even be pressure from certain factions for me to marry and raise the child with a father figure. Grandfather, these words are shallow to you right now, but I know deep in my soul that they will forever be true: Buck owns my heart, and he always will. I will occupy my time with raising our child and tending to the business of the Throne, and be happy with that. I cannot ask for more under these circumstances. But when Buck comes to visit, my heart will be full. And we will be happy. He will be known to our child, and I have no doubt that I could call on him for anything, at any time, and he would be here."

I hadn't thought of this in such specific terms. It brought an unfamiliar bulge to my throat. So I just nodded in consent to this arrangement.

"Jules, I don't say it enough, but I am so impressed with the person you are. I hope to live long enough to see the young Prince or Princess grow. It would be the most joy this old man could experience. You make me very happy and immensely proud."

We left the King knowing that everything we were doing was for the safety of the child, as we had committed to. But I was forlorn. Couldn't help it. It never occurred to me that I would ever be offered a chance for normalcy or consistency in my life. I never had any options before; I was alone. Worked alone, lived alone, traveled alone. Moved from place to place without ever establishing ties. And was fine with it all. Hell, I preferred it. But now I had discovered a part of me that craved something different. I wanted to raise this child. I wanted to be a husband to Jules. And not in any general sense; but in the specific sense that these two people were a part of me. And would be forever.

CHAPTER 62

Everything was set. I would fly off into the sunset on the King's jet. The flight plan was for Greece again, so it wouldn't raise any suspicions. But the final destination would not be known until after take-off, when I inform the pilot. The desire to stay with Jules and see her through this was a burning one. Of all the difficult things I have done in my life, this tops the list. But even I am not selfish enough to stay. I am grateful for the time we had, and looking forward to the next time we will be together.

Jules wants to go along on the flight, but that gives her knowledge that can only put her in danger. As it is, I'm making the pilot land on a desert strip I know about in the middle east. It borders three Countries, so he probably won't even know what Country he lands in for sure. He most certainly will have no way to track me from there. That's as good as I can do with a jet. Were it a plane, I would parachute somewhere into the darkness and he would have but a guess as to where I landed. But it would have been close to here. Iraq was one of those three bordering Countries.

And there was some bad guy in Iraq that needed to be gone.

Jules and I spend our last day wandering on the palace grounds. We stroll through the stables and the gardens, and have a simple lunch by a brook that flowed through the property. We talk about the baby, the King, the future; everything. I watched her intently all day. I had never got used to her beauty; and have never taken any part of her for granted.

It was a perfect day.

At dusk, she took me to the airfield. Her security force followed us, as always. Sesia and Wan had asked for the duty that evening. They broke with procedure and hugged me on the tarmac. "If ever you need anything..." was all they could get out. Then they left. Brothers in arms. Nothing like it.

Jules and I held each other for a minute. I pulled back and put my hand on her stomach. I held her eyes for another few seconds and embraced her again. I needed to remember how this felt. I had the feeling this memory would get me through some lonely times to come. Words had already passed between us that let her know what she was to me; what we were to each other. There was no more to say. She smiled at me; I couldn't find one. She's still the strongest person I know. I walked up the steps and turned for one last look at the best two things that ever happened to me.

EPILOGUE
One Year Later

I was feeling an excitement that I simply was not used to—maybe had never even experienced. Just a few minutes more. We had a smooth landing, but I didn't notice. I almost couldn't wait for the airstairs to roll up to the door. We had kept in touch—frequently—via secure means of communication. But I had not seen Jules in a year. And had never seen Starr. This would be a banner day for me.

Jules and Starr met me at the bottom of the steps. Jules reached and gave me a fierce hug. I thought she was going to crush the baby between us, and tried to make some space. "Don't crush the baby!"

Jules smiled. "Don't worry. She's tough, like her Daddy."

I couldn't wait any longer. She handed Starr to me. I held her gingerly and looked down through misty eyes. "And she's beautiful, like her Mommy."

END

www.ingramcontent.com/pod-product-compliance
Lightning Source LLC
LaVergne TN
LVHW011816060526
838200LV00053B/3804